HOBOKEN CAPTAINS, FORE AND AFT

by

M.A. O'Brien

ISBN: 978-0-7596-2108-4 (sc)
ISBN: 978-0-7596-2107-7 (e)

Print information available on the last page.

This book is printed on acid free paper.

1stBooks – rev. 6/12/01

Title; HOBOKEN CAPTAINS, FORE AND AFT

by M.A. O'Brien

Song of the Shanty Man

"Transported I am, from the haunts of man
on the banks of the Hudson Stream,
Where the wolves and the owls, and their
menacing howls, disturb our nightly dream."

Thus sang the first ferry master, as he rowed the flat barge that served as Revolutionary transportation up and down the mighty Hudson. His was a dry and thirsty occupation, and he was constantly assailed by strange sights and sounds from both sides of the Hudson.

River pirates abounded and shanty gangs with names like "the Down-river Cowboys," and "the Upriver Continental Bully Boys", were a prevalent part and parcel of our aquatic history and culture.

Both sides of the river boasted rowdy late night revelers, who over time generously donated their nightly contributions to the pickling of early American living.

Our early Hoboken, no stranger to the liquid refreshment culture and accompanying thirst of the nation had earned its place in history. A historical tribute, much of which, excluding baseball and the birth place of Frank Sinatra, has not been publicly revealed.

Baseball, after all was a landlubber sport, except for an occasional fly ball into the river, and Frank, after all was Frank.

Since there must have been an aquatic beginning, this author has subscribed, temporarily to the maxim, that wetter is better, and has stretched an historical curiosity all the way back to a sober Hoboken, where this author must apologetically remain. This present non politically correct position, however, is certainly not mandatory for the reader.

Shortly before previous gentrifications and the mowing of the newly invented steamboat wheel of progress over our predecessors, a new upward Hoboken emerged.

A wandering local poet, in love with Hoboken and the written word, described her in detail, "as an aging Madam with a face lift". For it's time it was an accurate caricature, but she is now viewed as being less sober, more educated by travel and culture, and infinitely more gastronomical. Her manners have declined, and are now deplorably attached to her greed. Yet, as her waistline has expanded so have we.

The Ship's Log of the Half Moon…kept by the first mate of the voyage, Robert Juet, also contained a surveyors map, hand drawn in 1600, by Johnathon Prinz and Thomas Holmes, navigators and surveyors of the Dutch West (later East) India Company.

It was bordered on all four sides by imaginary sea monsters, and incredible strange animals which became the bait that lured Lord Michael Pauw (Pavonia) in Holland, to purchase, sight unseen, the local area of land covering Hoboken, Jersey City, and Weehawken. Pauw was viewing, for the first time, the oldest known sight of the Jersey Shore.

The high ground, in the extreme left corner is Castle Point. Pauw had read the Half Moon's ship's previous voyages with interest, and had recorded several statements that particularly impressed him in his personal journal.

"September 2, five on the clock", we anchored in that great lake of water, and fished for our food."

They caught nothing.

September 4…after moving the ship further off the Hoboken Cove, they "Caught ten great mullets, of a foot and a half long apiece, and a ray, as great as four men could haul in the ship."

Unable to cook the food on the wooden ship, they rowed ashore, and shared their catch with two braves who suddenly had climbed out of the nearby trees.

This became the earliest surviving record of a seafood dinner, with friends and neighbors, on the Jersey shore!

Pauw was also instrumental in befriending the Quakers, and hiring DeVries as Captain of "The King David", the first settlers to arrive in Hoboken, and was present, himself, aboard the first arriving ship.

He was already versed in the customs and totems of each tribe, and knew some of their language, and their differing trade dialects. He was present at the Dutch Directors meetings, of the East India Company, as they smoked their long pipes of tobacco, and plotted their fortunes to be made in "The New Amsterdam."

Pauw's friends, Jan Evertson Boot and Michael Jansen, were already heroes to the group, and were living among the Indians peacefully and "had the respect and trust of their brethren of the woods."

Pauw was not altogether unprepared when he sailed on the King David.

Two in transit occurrences were noted on said ship. The death of a crew member and burial at sea. (Henry Jacobs, consumption} and the birth of a female child to the wife of Henrik Van Vorst, just before the ship docked at Hoboken Cove. The proud parents named her "Liberty."

A son was born the following year in Jersey City at the land that Pauw owned, at "Ahasimus" (Jersey City) He was named David, as the New Netherlands presented itself as a Goliath to the scripturally significant Quakers, and perhaps also as an honorable tribute to the Captain.

These nine Quaker men, their seven wives, and two new children became the government and the first documented settlers here. A second ship, under Captain May, later brought another thirty citizens.

Two of the crew members, Van Vorst and Van Vleck became Justices of the Peace and Judges. Nicholas Varlet and Aert Teunessen Van Putten, built the first brewery here, and sold the first beer on tap.

They were later scalped by the natives, and the brewery eventually became big business. It was also a constant source of annoyance to the Quakers and some of the more tea totalling citizens.

Hudson's SECOND voyage here has an additional interesting log comment. It mentioned the fact that a keg of beer was unloaded the first time the Indians met the white men, and the Chief, "Was foameing at he mouthe, and fallinge downe drunken". It said as soon as he was able to be sober, he ordered more beer...

On May 12, 1668, Bayard, (pre-Stevens) bought the property, and the Brewhouse which the Dutch had built for their beer, was still an active part of the culture and economy.

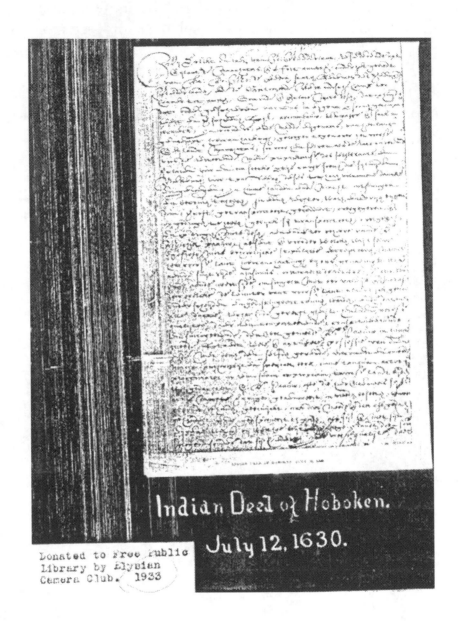

Indian Deed of Hoboken.
July 12, 1630.

Psalm 107

"they that go down to the sea in ships, that do business in mighty waters, they view the works of the Lord, and his wonders in the deep." vs. 23

Book One

M.A. O'Brien

CHAPTER ONE
CAPTAIN STEWART DEAN

Seventeenth century pioneers spent their life's blood carving out a meager existence, taming the landscape and multiplying. A bag of flour, a good wagon or plow horse, or a workable river raft was   priceless treasure in this valley wilderness.

Quaker neighbors, assisted by natives, shared farm implements and etched out homesteads from acres of forest. Personal belongings were precious and homemade skills evolved to etch the culture and color the century "blue." Whatever dishes or kitchen utensils survived the sea voyage were 'delft 'stoneware from Holland, usually blue and painted with scenes of Windmills and other geographical places of interest. There was much labor and little leisure, but time was always made for a "meeting," a sunrise ceremony, on the shore, to ask the blessings of Providence on incoming ships.

In the very beginning of the Quaker culture ships were few and far between, thus were early heroes made of Captains. Commerce and trade, and sometimes booty crisscrossed the Atlantic, and sea bells and lonely church bells tolled for shipwrecks, missing husbands and relatives.

News from relatives in Holland, necessary pioneer staples, and holds that contained cargoes of bolts of cloth, seeds for planting, and tools for building were much in demand. Fierce and bitter valley winters added to the adventure of early Colonial living, and a variety of cold weather illness claimed many. Ships were eagerly awaited and the Captain and crew were honored and treated with the utmost of respect. It was not uncommon to "take the "crewboys" in" and in exchange for sea stories and voyage tales, the lucky young cabin boys would be plied with Dutch pies and roasted puddings and hot breads and sweetmeats from the zoftig wives of the pioneers. Dutch candle making, bread baking, quilting and legends melded with the talents of the pottery, copper pipes, and beadwork of the natives in the Dutch "kuchens", Sea stories abounded and thus, in this manner were legends and heroes made, and commerce and trade increased.

Weeks and sometimes months went by between ships. Nevertheless, spotted outposts of colonial colonies formed along the Hudson. Some, like the Quakers were organized into helpful groups, and "The Society of Friends", the Quakers, flourished, with help from "their brethren of the woods."

Trappers and fur traders and prospectors frequented the shore in home-made lees and shelters independent of the status quo and the biblical strict culture of the inland dwellers. They were called "seaborder people" and "pondshiners,' and although fed, on occasion, were mostly avoided by the churchgoing public. They "squatted" at the Cave of Echoes (Sybil's Cave), lived off the land, and traded and scavenged whenever necessary. Superstition, not uncommon in Dutch culture thus evolved. Whispers of witches and German gnomes mixed with sea stories, Irish legends and Native beliefs, and a whole culture of new superstition abounded.

The high seas were rife with salty tales of travel, and these merged, also into the vocabulary of the land. The natives continued their commerce on the Elk trails, and also awaited the coming ships. "Reena Moholo", a great boat or ship, and "Keeko Gull Une", How much will you pay for this?, were new words spoken and signed. No trading ritual was accomplished by either the "pondshiners" or the braves, without "minnie pishbee" a small beer. Kegs of strong Dutch Beer were put up for trade, and the first ramshackle brewery was already under construction by a settler named Nicholas Varlet. The tea totaling Quakers were properly incensed, but were busy farming, and harvesting and learning from the natives which barks, berries and native plants were useful for medicine.

Back in England, under Royal guardianship, a new alliance was in the planning stages. Gentry Lords and Ladies, anxious to cash in on the fur trading and untold riches of the Hudson Valley pawned their jewels, sold their lands and began to finance sea voyages and worthy captains. One such financier was Henry 11, also known as the Duc Du Guise.Political infighting with Louis XIII's prime minister had caused the Duc to fall from favor at court. He was most flamboyant with ostrich plumes in his hat, a steel gorget around his throat to guard him under his lace collar, and a bachelor lovelock, a curl grown longer than his full head of hair, which sported ribbons belonging to his lady friends at court. His demeanor was such that Van Dyck the Flemish painter was commissioned to do a painting of him in 1633. This was fortunate for both Van Dyck and the Duc, as within a few days of the painting the Queen had him poisoned. His lands, inheritance and investments of ship's voyages were then confiscated at his death, at the Queen's request, and the choosing of Captains followed.

Expertise at sea, and experience were part and parcel of the choosing of the Captains, who were rewarded liberally with newly built ships and newly coined monies, and then pointed in the direction of "the new world." Intensive interviews and investigations were conducted for Captains. "The India Company of Experiment" was formed, and financed, and later, as profits expanded split into factions of East and West and other worthy titles, and expanded to other countries.

There were many worthy Captains. Such a one admired by both the Royalty of the times and the Colonial Settlers and natives was Hoboken Captain Stewart Dean. Although not considered as highly favored, and presented with a galleon as others of his time, this gentle Quaker was given an 80 ton 6 gun square rigged loop, which he christened, "The Experiment."

His precious charter in hand, and crew awaiting, Captain Dean cleared New York Harbor, on his maiden voyage in the deep winter of 1785. On December the Eighteenth, in less than enthusiastic winter weather, and some ice forming 'in the inland tide" the good captain set sail for Antigua, and the surrounding tropical area. In July of the same year, good news reached the investors, that the "Experiment" was indeed spotted in Antigua, and had docked for trade and commerce.

Aboard was a smiling and prayerful Captain Dean who posted a letter of appreciation to the ever worried investors.

Eighteen months went by and the celebration of "the India Company of Experiment" began to wane. Verbal proliferation and seaman's solemn accounts of mouth gossip of voyages, contained no word of "the Experiment, " nor was there any message from Captain Dean. The investors decided to cover their losses, and look to other sources of revenue. They tried to sell their shares in the ship's bounty, but the scuttlebutt of the local sea faring culture prevented them, and they simply, and sadly went on to other business.

The Colonial inhabitants spoke softly and prayed gently for the good Captain and his two cabin boys which were familiar faces and well liked here. The crew was mostly unknown to them, but Little Tom, a part Indian orphan, and Black Jack, the son of a slave were part and parcel to this area and well known to the locals. Many a colonial candle burned low befriending these two lads, and their tales of local barge voyages, and Indian stories were legendary. Both could read and write a little, a fact well utilized by Captain Dean, when he searched out the area for Cabin Boys. It was common practice for a newly appointed Captain to search the seacoast and surrounding wharves for hire, and Hoboken, having a large Quaker following, was no exception.

Thus, no mother or citizen was want to complain as the Captain rowed across the Hudson with his two new seamen in tow, and boarded his Experiment in New York Harbor. Cabin boys were well treated by good Captains, and fame and fortune awaited those willing to be educated "on the tides." Shipboard life was hard and busy, but there was always some time for education amidst the life at sea. That year, in the home port, the winter was especially fierce, and the scarcity of necessities was an ever presenting problem. Little Tom and Black Jack were simply two less mouths to feed, but were continually remembered at Sunday meetings and in prayers.

A year and a half passed, and within that eighteen months more immigrants arrived. A town of homemade Colonial hand hewn houses sprung up. and the population doubled with incoming settlers. Crops and farming were flourishing, the Indians were still befriending the Colonials, for the most part, and the new town boasted a bakery, a market and a small trading store, alongside the brewery. A wooden church was constructed near the shore, and one enterprising trip had brought an oversized ship's bell which served as the church bell to ring out the news of approaching ships. The town crier, hired by the town fathers had less to announce, as the beginnings of a newspaper "the Observer" were evolving. Except for an occasional trapper or surveyor there was very little in the way of ornaments or material goods, with the exception of candles and homespun.

The Experiment and Captain Dean and his cabin boys and crew became a sad memory in the minds and hearts of the busy settlers.

On the Fourth Of June in the Year 1897 the bell of the Quaker church pealed and pealed. Spotted on the horizon and still incoming was a ship in full sail. As it passed the Cave of Echoes it's Captain was heard singing, and the echo of his melodious sea chant was heard and repeated all over town. Scoped, on board and assisting the captain were two cabin boys. Taller and exhibiting more dignity than most of the sailors on board, were Little Tom and Black Jack.

Their hair was pigtailed in a strange manner, and they were dressed in the finest softest shiniest material, most unlike homespun. Each wore a conical hat, and their black pantaloons were such that they waved in the slightest breeze. Their bright shirts and shoes were embroidered with the most intricate sea dragons in striking colors.

Word of their arrival spread like wild fire through the Colony…

Overwhelming curiosity joined with shouts of welcome as Quakers, farmers and the few remaining Indians lined up on the dock. Gentleman investors and PatRoons stood quietly off to the sidelines as the noisy crowd waited. Cheers and a-hoys were hollered from all points of the shore, as the good Captain's ship, in glorious full sail, glided slowly past. As he neared the cave of Echoes and trimmed the sails he sang a strange sing song sea chant in a language never heard before on the Colonial shores of Hoboken.

Some enterprising musicians had formed a musical trio and were playing whatever homemade contrived instruments they could find, in order to welcome the returning vessel. Upon tying up at the dock, the crew, with as much pomp and dignity as ceremoniously possible began carting and carrying chest upon chest of bounty to the willing dock. Several chests were opened for inspection, and thrown to view were huge bolts of yellow and gold striped silk, accompanied by satins of both plain and ornately embroidered nature. The crowd, oohing and aahing at every article, cheered and wondered at these strange and wonderful treasures. The maroon embroidered silk was especially admired, the giant smoking pipes were viewed with much comment and curiosity, and some of the articles were so very strange, their usage had to be explained to the crowd of colonial onlookers,

Most amazing were the dishes and cups and bowls. Each was examined and found to be so fine and translucent and beautiful, that when asked what it was called, the seamen, not as adept at the language as the captain and cabin boys, could only remember the name of it's place of origin and port of call, "China."

Giant ginger jars and urns joined the display, and while the crowd admired the booty, Captain Dean officially invited the city fathers, who were present aboard to his own personal cabin. Carefully escorted through the noisy throng by the cabin boys, the city fathers boarded. They stood, mouth's agape as they entered the Captain's cabin. Never, had they seen anything so entrancing. Hundreds of lit ginger jar lamps, in differing sizes, each boasting it's own design and translucent colors lit amazing tapestries of Dragons which hung from walls and ceilings. A huge, hand drawn map, with intricately designed trees and mountains decorated the Captain's main wall. It covered the entire wall and upon close inspection was found to be hand embroidered in gilded silken threads. There were mountains and clouds and three tiered Pagodas, in predominately red and green colorations. In an ornately embroidered wing chair, covered with green intertwined dragons, and to the left of the map, sat the first Chinese man in Colonial America.

Judging by size he was about four feet tall. Pigtailed, silken robed in an ornate red and gold jacket, with black frog closures, he sat like a statue in the chair. At a nod from the captain, he stood, his feet encased in tiny embroidered black slippers, compressed his hands together in a prayerful position, and bowed. The Captain, speaking in sing song dialect, waved his hand and the amazing little man, still bowing and smiling, quickly disappeared into the galley part of the ship, much to the shocked amazement of the inhabitants.

Within a few short weeks, only the very poorest of the valley kept candles, as ginger jar lamps were soon boasted about and displayed in most Colonial homes. The era of the Whale Oil Lamp, the Calumet smoking pipe, and the melting pot of new immigrants from foreign shores had begun.

Captain Dean made seven more trips to China, and over the next few years, along with other seafarers, provided much in the way of progress of possessions for the Colonists. A new age of commerce had begun, and another first in Hoboken History was carefully recorded with the oncoming tide, as the treasures and wonders of Canton became familiar to the Colonies.

Captain Dean and his cabin boys aged gracefully here in Hoboken, and in his pre-retiring years, he sailed many a tourist and Lord and Lady past the cave of Echoes into nearby ports of commerce. Always with a song in his heart, sometimes in Chinese, he sailed upriver on personal charter trips with the tourists. Eventually he began to complain that the open sea was shrinking. The nearby ports of call in Long Island and Manhattan were becoming crowded with overzealous tourists. The price of fame and the new vogue of the ever busy Hudson Valley included a charter ride on The Experiment with the infamous Captain Dean. It was considered the epitome of importance and style to be invited to the Captain's Cabin for a dinner engagement, and of course, an exhilarating conversation of sea tales.

Eventually the good Captain was quoted as saying that he longed for a quiet inland life, in a real home on sturdy ground, away from the sea and it's magic. This new strain of thought was exacerbated by his frequent new problems with the cabin boys. They were now grown, and were considerable men of means, and frequently lived among the gentry. Dutch Masters, now in charge, were beginning to exact tax on anything seaworthy, and there were constant accompanying squabbles with the immigrants and the tourists and remaining few Indians.

Most of the new problems centered on Dutch Superstition, which had somehow most mysteriously evolved among the inhabitants. Whispers of Witches Covens surrounded the Cave of Echoes, and the Seaborder people and the pondshiners were consistent victims concerning the same. The Dutch Masters and their lackeys had a peculiar habit, upon the death of one of their own. Perhaps the guilt of their taking tax advantage of the locals had somehow interrupted their psyche and bred strange fears.

Wakes were spent in grim silence "waiting for the token." A knock, a strange sound, a far away howl was interpreted as meaning that the newly deceased was in some way suffering on his way to eternity, and wanted the living, who remained, to know it. The dead, it was believed could somehow warn the living, and perhaps, if a past grudge was not settled here, could bring some harm to those involved. This evolved the Quaker custom of placing coins over the closed eyes of the deceased.

Consequently, most full moons were feared and the high tide, the slow tide that surfaces by undercover currents at the cresting moon was renamed "The Witches Tide." Fireflies, their lights aglow, lighted on the masts of ships in the strange blue moonlight, and the fish, including sturgeon, here, grew to enormous size. It was not uncommon to spot three hundred pound sturgeon splashing and diving in Hoboken Cove, or to view an occasional whale.

More superstition abounded in the Advent of Salem, and the label of strange or supernatural was attached to all odd occurrences. Triskadaiephobia reigned rampantly among the Dutch Masters. The sailor's ancient fear of the number thirteen took on a new life of it's own. As far back as Columbus, it was considered bad luck to start a voyage on a Friday, especially if it fell on the Thirteenth of the month. This cultural phenomena, mixed with the new noises from the cave of Echoes, and the ghosts who now roamed among the living who were "waiting for a token."

Captain Dean had seen superstition at sea, and with his ever present Bible under his arm, had mostly dispelled it as nonsense to the satisfaction of everyone on board. Many Dutch now considered him an example, and allayed their fears by sleeping with their Bibles under their pillows. Many still claimed to hear strange sounds at night.

Captain Dean was becoming increasingly uneasy as silly superstition increased and abounded. His cabin boys, now men, who occasionally assisted him in charters with the tourists and locals, were consistently adding to the problems concerning the same. Each took every available opportunity to capitalize, for profit, on the fears of the citizens.

Not so Little Tom, who was now a Captain of his own business charter, and was rarely in local port, preferring instead, the warmer waters, and sunny climate of the Caribbean. However, BlackJack remained, dressed in fine clothes, and spent his existence frequenting local taverns and assisting the growing gentry in pursuit of their many activities and pleasures. It was whispered he owned and managed an Opium den.

Publicly, he had most personal knowledge of the haunts and habits of most of the townfolk, and he did become, after the fashion of his peers, steeped in greed, and most untrustworthy. Rarely was he now available for the good Captain for a charter, or a short trip upriver for Colonial needs, unless it was to his abject financial benefit. He was often in minor scrapes with the Dutch Masters, but each time, somehow managed to extricate himself from the trouble at hand. His cardplaying skills at the game that bore his name became legendary, as well as both "apothecary shops" run by Chinese immigrants that served the Dutch well with medicines. Laudanum and Opium syrups were especially in demand for various illnesses and complaints.

One particular incident, and his conduct decided the retirement and exodus of Captain Stewart Dean. A widow, Dame Boot, owned and maintained a piece of shoreline property with a small shack which bordered the woods. She was aging badly, bent and disheveled and in poor health from the "rheumatiz. She was rarely seen, except on occasion by a passing vessel, who viewed her from a distance, basket weaving with the few remaining natives, who lived at the edge of the river and kept mostly to themselves.

The good Captain, ever in search of new baskets to hold his catch of a day of fishing, occasionally visited this bent and twisted Dame, and always paid her a little extra, as a good Christian would do for her sustenance. Her baskets were well made, and he fished often off the bow, rarely missing the opportunity for a fine seafood dinner.

BlackJack had also visited the widow Boot, and was not above returning after dark to take without asking whatever goods he could find. When Dame Boot filed an official complaint, through a gentry tax agent, BlackJack branded her, by reputation, as a Witch. Widow Boot disappeared one day and was never heard from again.

Word of mouth escalated the frightened Dutch into a frenzy of gossip and fear. Dame Boot was seen riding over the smoking chimneys of the town hall on a broomstick. Her laugh was heard cackling in lit fireplaces among the logs, and a black cat was caught in town who was said to speak in her voice, if followed. BlackJack was questioned publicly by the town fathers, and in his own defense, swore he saw "star tracks around her shack," and described in vivid detail, stars marked into the ground near the entrance of her shack, surrounded by circles, which led strangely into the woods.

This occasion of superstitious scuttlebutt was too much for the aging Captain. He told his neighbors and friends that he had enough of the seacoast of Hoboken, and as promptly as possible retired to Arbor Hill, near Albany, New York. It was spoken that he lived to a very ripe old age, and was much respected and admired by his new townsfolk and neighbors.

M.A. O'Brien

Book Two

Captain David Pieterz DeVries
Hoboken, the First...

by M.A. O'Brien

M.A. O'Brien

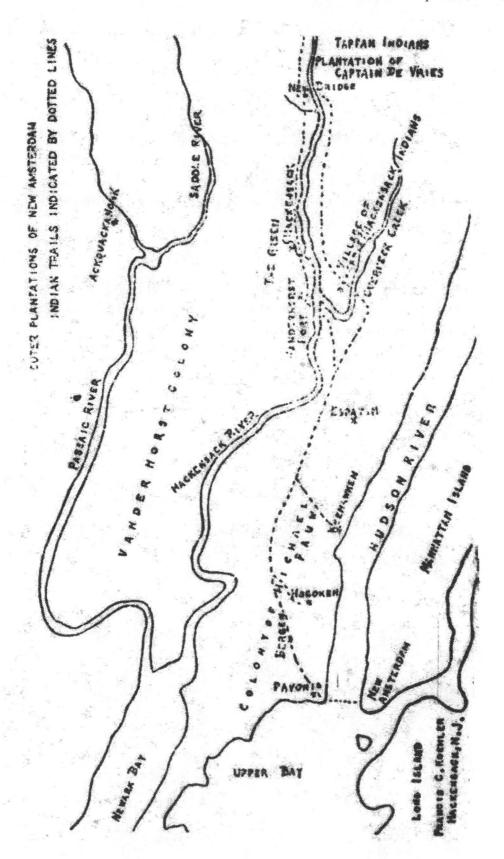

Our valley and the surrounding area have a hidden history of firsts that have not been generally acknowledged by the every day citizens who occupy it. Families of the children of men, driven always, by a personal quest for freedom, spent their existence and their lifes blood here in the Hudson Valley, only to hollow out a future for the rest of us. Our own Lenape, as they wished to be known, wanted only hunting space and the freedom to worship, yet they were slowly and progressively eradicated in the name and place of progress, this same grinding progress that affects us all. This book is composed in remembrance of all those unrecognized souls of our past pioneer empire, who previously walked, sailed warred or plowed their itinerant way across the pages of our history.

This is also a tribute to the noble red man of Hoboken, who counted seasons, stars and time by sleeps and moons, and who tred softly, in quiet hand made mocassins, to follow the hidden trail of the Elk. Credence must also be given to the local villains. They began their journey here, as men of good intentions, but by time and circumstance became poached in greed, and eventually succumbed to the most heinous acts of villainy. Heroes could not have been as accomplished without them, thus they are exemplified here, interspersed and parallel to the very heroes that they assisted to materialize, across the pages of time.

Chapter One

Hoboken, the Beginning

Our original history begins with one huge iced over continent which scientists in our time have named Pangeia. Eventually the ice age begins to thaw, and waterways and shorelines evolve, expand and rise from the tundra.

Migratory game, enjoying the new warmth and chasing their own food supplies, have crossed the land bridge. (Beringia)

Pliesticene (Stone age) man is migrating, as are the ancestors of the Lenape.

Archaeologists have labeled these immigrants "Paleo", a word that translates into "ancient".

Several Paleo campsites have been discovered near the Muscenetcong River in New Jersey, the Dutchess Quarry Cave, near Monroe, New York and the Shawnee Mini-sink Site near the Delaware Water Gap in Pennsylvania.

Many more have remained undiscovered!

Geologists have proven that this area was once tundra, and that cold adapted animals existed here in Paleo times. These included Wooly Mammoths, Musk Ox, Caribou, Moose, Elk, Seal and Walrus.

Life was extremely difficult in this bitter and hostile environment. Gradually the climate became warmer and dense forests began to grow. Small groups of natives flourished, organized, came together in groups and became hunters, fishers and gatherers. (C.A 800 - 1000 B.C.)

Our natives collectively made more efficient hunting tools and learned to cook their food. By approximately 500 A.D. the bow and arrow had replaced the spear, and the first crude lean to's appeared as dwellings.

Natives became canoe builders and exchanged wampum as currency. They also farmed their food. Burial mounds found by archaeologists suggest that there was a very real belief of life after death. Fruit was dried with meat in strips to provide a very chewy summer and winter Pemmican. Maize was grown, eaten stored and made into mush.

Anthropologists have collected tools, and weapons, which have been displayed in local museums as the history of the late woodland time (C A 900 -1600)

Thus as we move into the early 15th Century, tall ships with billowing sails, sponsored by overseas royalty, are just beginning to touch the shores of Hoboken for riches or trade routes.

"I remember that when I was a laughing boy I stood upon the sands of the great sea shore and saw a big white canoe with wings whiter than the Swans and wider than many Eagles, come from the rising Sun". In the canoe were many white men. Then the children of the Lenape were masters of the world. The salt lake gave us fish, the woodlands gave us the deer and the Elk, and the air gave us many birds. We took wives who bore us many children. We worshiped the Great Spirit. We kept the enemy beyond the sound of our hunting grounds."

Tamen Und Delaware Chief

Chapter Two

The Culture

"Hoboken Hocking" native Americans spoke Unami, a dialect of the Eastern Algonquian Delaware Nation. The natives who lived here spoke of themselves as "common" or "ordinary people." They had many affectionate names for the land that surrounded them, but none of them beheld ownership, as everything that had life belonged to the Great Spirit. Dances of celebration and festivals to celebrate life were held seasonally and accordingly, mostly at Harvest.

The October full Moon was called the Travelling Moon, and was a signal directly from the Great Spirit to move the tribe inland to their Winter Lodge at Communipaw (Avenue) now Jersey City. They wisely took their lodges, and their dried provisions and waited out the winter away from the icy river and frozen shoreline.

New Year's Eve was celebrated on the First Day of February, and began a week long festival with "singing and dancing and taking of wives."

The Full Moon in September was the Corn Dance. Maidens of marriagable age would dance at harvest to honor a spirit called Corn Woman.

Occasionally, as if on cue, Corn Woman would appear in the smoke of the celebratory camp fire, with a message of spiritual significance for the tribe. At this occasion the braves would choose their mates to be. Wooden whistles flutes and drums provided accompanying music.

The origin of Maize is still surrounded in mystery, yet it was a staple with beans and squash, in the native diet. During the harvest three beautiful maidens were dressed in their finest quill decorated deerskins, with feathers and wampum. They danced a thankful prayer to the Great Spirit. One represented Corn, one Beans and one Squash. It was called the Dance of the Three Sisters, and became a Lenape tradition.

Later accounts by Sea Captains (DeVries) who befriended the natives here mention specifically the Corn Dance Harvest Festival, and what a great honor it was to be invited to same.

The discovery in 1609 by the first mate of Henry Hudson's Half Moon was not the first mention of Hoboken, on this continent. Jean De Verazzano of Florence, Italy had passed through the area and docked in New York Harbor in 1524. His ship was loaded with Grape vines which were spoiling, which were a gift from the King to be planted in "the new world."

The Dutch were amazed to find "all manner of grapes and berries being carefully cultivated by the natives" when they arrived. From the very beginnings of Hoboken history, Grapes have played a part in culture and later art.

Other early references in ship's logs were made to "Hoebuck".

One especially commands attention and is listed in the log of Verazzano.

Esteveo Gomes, commanding a Portuguese man of War, captured 58 dark souls off the coast of Hoebuck and sold them as slaves in Spain.

He spied them on the shoreline digging, and assumed they were seeking Gold. It was custom for part of the tribe to dig on the shore for the sacred red clay and soapstone that the natives used to construct their sacred peace pipes…Hoboken Haak ING…the Land of the Sacred Pipe….was listed as HOPOCAN HAAKNG…in their language…Pipes eventually evolved into a whole culture and spread across the new land via trade routes.

There are genealogists in Spain who have found links to the Lenape and traced their ancestry to this area.

We study Hudon's THIRD voyage as history, disincluding the dark side of the voyages that involve the taking of slaves.

French and Canadian trappers were here long before the Dutch, but cleverly remained unrecorded. Game in this plentiful woodland paradise was plentiful, and the climate was as mild and friendly as the natives that occupied it.

There were other occurrences that had a lasting effect on our culture. The nearby Minsi Delawares were cultivating a plant which they considered very pleasant for smoking. They called it "Glanican". It assisted in the commerce of the pipes and many trades were fostered accordingly.

Later, "Glanican" and the Pipes were used in the burial rites of Mohawks, Oniedas Onandangas, Cayugas and Senecas, and were joined by the Tuscaroras in 1712, when a common trading language was adopted.

Munsi and Unami in our area provided the place names for towns (see Touching Leaves Woman)

Thick woodlands and pure waters afforded fine hunting, fishing and oysters. Sturgeon hunts resulted in catches weighing in at five hundred pounds.

One September entry, in the log of the Half Moon, describes twenty eight canoes, each fully bedecked with furs, oysters and beans, approaching the great ship for trade.

This powerful flotilla was led by the medicine man and Chief of the entire region, Oratam.

Oratam was born in 1577 on the Elk Trail near Awapaugh Creek, (Overpeck) Creek. He was said to possess intimate knowledge of the entire area, and claimed kinship with the Great Spirit to whom all things belonged.

Oratam's overwhelming generosity sparked a legend here. He fell in love with a Dutch Widow, named Sarah Kierstede, adopted her into his tribe, and made her a gift of the land actually occupied by the main tribe of his relatives. It is today known as Hackensack.

Sarah Kierstede was chastised by the Dutch Masters for befriending the Indians, and feeding them, her husband killed, and her farm burned. Oratam found her wandering in the woods, still charred from trying to save here belongings, and took her to the Lenapes. She remained and befriended DeVries and several activists who were trying to help the natives (See later chapters)

Previous interactions of trade throughout the area had expanded the earliest foot paths and Elk trails, and today we walk Washington Street, following yet the wandering path of the long forgotten Elk. (see map 1638 Indian villages and Elk Trails)

Wooden mallets, stone chisels, and axe heads survive from this time in history. Villages dotted two prominent locations, in Hoboken and Weehawken. Drum messages and smoke signals fostered trade and the natives could actually view each other from two vantage points.

Lookouts stationed at Promontory Point (where an antique cannon now resides) could scout the river from the trees, and spot the war canoes of the fierce Manahattics or Canarsees. These enemies frequently forded the Hudson for raids and prisoners. Capturing the scalplock or the squaw of an enemy was a fortune of war, and sponsored many a brave's campfire tale.

Trade interacted, as tribes exchanged home grown Maize from Weehawken, (the Land of Maize) or trapped snakes from Siskake (Secaucus) to use for decorative or religious ritual.

Trails expanded to include powwows where tails of tall ships were exchanged, and verbal inventory was taken of objects worthwhile for trading.

New expressions entered the Native vocabulary, by way of the Dutch ships.

"Reeno Moholo" a great boat or ship.

"Keeko Gull Une?" How much will you pay for this? and the infamous

"Husko Purso Tospahala", very sick or near death, were several.

Three sons of the Iriquois, possibly and most probably of Oratam, "sold" Hoboken to the willing Dutch settlers for trinkets. The Deed was noted and recorded on July 12, 1630.
Later Centennials honored this action.

Kegs of beer accompanied trade, and the first ramshackle brewery was built by Nickolas Vaarlet. "Minnie Pishbee" accompanied all trades and later wars burned nearly all of Hoboken, but never a torch touched a brewery.

Pelting brought a rich fur trade, crops were cultivated, and soon the eager Dutch immigrants, well versed by the natives were farming and harvesting their own crops of Maize Beans, Squash and Pumpkins.

The natives also taught which barks and berries were useful for medicine, and how to rightfully use foodstuffs and shelter.

Gradually life improved for all, as more and more ships sail's were seen docking at the shore line.

Eventually and inevitably, a culture collision resulted. The Dutch pioneer mentality was to own land. The natives believed it could be used, "rented" and replaced. The Lenape were a spiritual people, even toward the killing of game, which was totally necessary for their survival.

A prayer apology was sent to the Great Spirit and no part of the animal was wasted or went unutilized.

Unscrupulous traders or privateers began to cheat the trusting natives, and added insult to injury by introducing whiskey into the trading rituals. This act fueled animosities and atrocities on both sides. It offended the Quakers, destroyed the natives resistance with the illness of alcoholism, and assisted the mindset to cheat the warriors out of everything possible.

Relationships deteriorated!

This era opened a portal in history for heroes and villains.

Chapter Three

DeVries

There are many who deserve a place of honor and recognition in our pioneer history.

Early pioneer writer and Sea Captain David Pieterz DeVries was such a man. He was also a Quaker!

Early quotes in sixteenth century pioneer journals and surveyor's logs (Johnathon Prinz, Thomas Holmes) explain that Captain DeVries, a Patroon, was justly awarded, through bravery in action, the property we now know as Staten Island.

DeVries befriended the natives here, and became a staunch supporter of the rights of the red man. He started the unknown and controversial practice of hiring the natives for pay to clear and farm his land.

He also wrote a book on the mistreatment of the natives, which he sent to the King of Holland, pleading for justice and payment for them.

DeVries was also a self appointed arbitrarian and was well known in pioneer circles as a fair man to judge and settle the frequent local disputes.

His ship that he captained to bring the settlers here was named "The King David." A ship's log passenger list written under his name as Captain reads:

Captain David Pieterz DeVries
Henry Jacobs
Gerrit Gerritsen
Dirk Clausen
Nickolas Vaarlet (later scalped, built the first brewery)
Henrik Van Vorst
Aert Teunissen Van Putten (built the first brewery at Sandy Hook) also scalped
Willem Kiest (the first Governor of New Jersey- appointed by the King of Holland, and the first Villain)
Tillman Van Vleck
Michael Paulusen (later bought Paulus Hook) and their wives and children

A later ship via the King David, brought the Schuyler, Van Deveer, Van Deusen Van Horne, DeWitt, Cabot, Clausen, Sanderson, Van Putten and Van Dyke families.

They bought eight farm lots, and three plantations here to grow tobacco for the East India Trading Company.

In exchange they were honor bound to supply "fifty people for each lot, a fully stocked farm with seed, a Pastor and a schoolmaster for the pioneer children."

Later, in history, Dutch slang slightly changed the terminology and coined each plot of land a "bouries", (bowery).

The land was also sized…

Settlers filled the spaces and as more white sails arrived with the sunrise, the native uprisings became more frequent and violent.

The buying and selling of land offended the natives with the year 1630 being recorded as especially significant. Michael Pauw (Pavonia) bought Hopokan, and Ahasimus (Jersey City).

Chapter Four

Kieft (pronounced Keest)
The First Governor

Into this powderkeg and uneasy setting a titled Director General was appointed by the Dutch rulers. Thus in 1638, Willem Kieft (pronounced Keest) sailed with strict orders from his mentors to "subdue the heathen redskins, in the name of the King, or wipe them from the face of the earth."

Well paid with a huge quantity of Dutch Guilders, and the commission of his own ship, which he named The Princess, he set sail immediately for Hoboken. Kiest was the ultimate villain. He enjoyed the reputation of a strict disciplinarian, and was not above displaying extreme cruelty to enforce his iron directives.

Several ship's references of this era show sailors hanging upside down from the yardarm to enforce discipline, while the good Captain had them beaten with planks. Shipboard discipline was fierce and the ship's doctors filed complaints continuosly "He not only practices cruelty, he enjoys it!" wrote one doctor on the Princess and then attempted to scratch his words out.

Governor Kieft's first official act upon landing, was to tax the natives and trappers on their furs, maize and wampum. This to them was unheard of and they refused to pay.

The good governor retaliated by holding in readiness a well paid goon squad of fully armed soldiers who would gleefully enforce whatever he wished.

Captain DeVries, organized a small group of settlers and farmers and paid his respects to the new governor. He stayed long and explained that the local natives were peaceful with the exception of an incident that had just occurred.

Marauding Mohawks were looting and killing on this side of the river, and raids were becoming continuous.

Kiest reiterated with his vow to wipe all of the redskins off the face of the earth. He unrolled plans for a massacre at Pavonia!

Stop this unholy work," begged DeVries, "you wish to break the mouths of the indians but you will also murder your own nation".

Kieft's final statement was to send his goon squad to Pavonia.

Drumbeats preceded them, and by the time the settlers who accompanied DeVries had returned to their farms, their families had been massacred and their farms burned by the warring tribes.

Meanwhile the peaceful Hoboken Lenape, banding with the neighboring Munsi from Weehawken fled for protection to the fort at Amsterdam.

They were turned away!

They returned to Pavonia, and buried their weapons as a gesture of peace.

The date was February 25, 1643, and the newly promoted Kieft, armed and leading a company of soldiers, massacred every one of the sleeping natives in a dawn attack.

Word travelled to the warring natives elsewhere, and their collective retaliation was both immediate and swift. A killing spree resulted and the shoreline and inner perimeter was burned all the way from Caven Point to Hoboken.

Captain DeVries, who in contemplating the seriousness of the coming slaughter could not sleep.

"I remained that night at the Governors to await his return to reason with him. I heard loud shrieks and went out to the parapets of the fort. I looked toward Pavonia, and saw nothing but the flash of guns, and heard nothing more of the yells and clamor of the indians who were butchered in their sleep." Captain David DeVries

"Some came running to us from the country having their hands cut off, some who had their legs cut off, were supporting their entrails with their arms, while others were mangled in other horrid ways, in part too shocking to be conceived."

"These wretches still did not know, as well as some of our own people did not know, but "thought" they had been attacked by the Mohawks."

Some of the Quakers tried to save a few children but were butted by the soldiers and did not succeed. Isaak Abrahamson, a Hebrew Captain, who owned and provided perhaps unknowingly, the vessels that were used and was told to await their return "saved" a little boy and hid him under the sail. Toward morning the child, overcome with hunger and cold, made some noise. Instantly "he was heard by the soldiers, dragged from under the sail, in spite of the endeavors of the skipper, was cut in two and thrown overboard".

This DeVries later recorded sarcastically, "as a feat worthy of ancient Rome."

Great was the rejoicing on Manhattan, by the Dutch when the soldiers returned bearing the ghastly heads of some of the victims as trophies of this brilliant military move.

Some of the new widows kicked the heads of the vanquished around the Fort in glee!

The Quakers, led by DeVries and others called a fast, and dressed in sorrow and mourning for church. At their prayer meeting they asked for direction from their God, and called for an end to revenge in all men.

After many hours of praying it was common for their presiding pastor to prophesy words directly from their God.

"The villainy you teach me, I will execute: and it shall go hard, but I will better the instruction." said the Prophet.

The warring natives began a new tactic of warfare. They were never seen, and accomplished their destruction not generally by open warfare, but by creeping through the bush and setting fire to the roofs, which were constructed of either reeds or straw.

So thoroughly was their destruction accomplished that from Taeppen to the Highlands, the country was once more in possession of the original masters. "we huddle in poverty together, where we are not one hour safe", wrote a settler sequestered at the Fort.

Seven nations had joined together for war on the whites, and the drumbeats were continuous.

Within hearing distance of the drums was Captain DeVries. He had organized the remaining settlers and farmers and legally and formally charged Governor Kiest with misgovernment. The paperwork, containing written complaints and instances of abuse, was sent to the King of Holland.

Kiest received a letter from the King. He was ordered back to Holland for trial, and would be personally required to defend his administration at court.

His ship, the Princess, overloaded with all of his collected booty, sunk in a storm off the coast of Wales. He, and his family and friends, together with all of his possessions were drowned. Unwilling and unable to throw the booty overboard to save the ship, it went down in the storm!

Upon the absence of the Governor, Captain DeVries took temporary charge. He began negotiations to ransom several prisoners from the natives taken in raids. He freed many, among the first was a child, Ide Van Vorst, who was taken when his farm was burned.

An uneasy peace prevailed for a time, and many immigrants awaited peace within the safety of the Fort at New Amsterdam.

May 11 1647 a new Governor was "appointed" to replace the missing Kiest. His name was Peter Stuyvesant, and his forte was to fill up this land with as many settlers as possible.

Back in Holland, he was assisted by the Dutch West Indies (later East) Company. It granted it's chief Constable the land we know as Bayonne and call Constable Hook. White residents cleared and farmed the area we call Greenville. The Indians were furious as this land mass was "Minkakwa", their best hunting ground. They immediately warred and took some captives.

This was soon to become the fame of Gen. Stuyvesant. His finest hour in history had him showing great wisdom and courage. He personally met with the chiefs of the local tribes, at their main camp in Hackensack, and set up future negotiations and treaties. He ransomed the captives, and made an offer to purchase the entire land mass from the natives.

A massive powwow was finally agreed upon and on January 30, 1658, nine Hackensack Chiefs, including Oratam, in their finest ceremonial dress canoed to the new council room at Fort Amsterdam. (New York City)

Each made their mark on a document giving the "white eyes" all the land covering Hackensack, North Hudson, Weehawken, Secaucus, West New York, Bayonne, Jersey City and Hoboken. The last boundary of ownership stretched all the way to The Kill Van Kull.

The original deed, preserved by the State House in New York, lists the price of these lands.

80 Fathoms of Wampum
20 Fathoms of Cloth
12 Brass Kettles
Guns
Blankets
and a half a keg of Beer

A lasting peace had finally prevailed.

Stuyvesant, capitalizing on the new found peace, searched out a new defensible site on which to build a town square. He wanted a jewel. He needed a new stockaded centerpiece for the many arriving new immigrants.

His surveyor, Jacques Cortelyou, marked out four blocks where the view of the Palisades offered both protection and a showcase. This act began early Bergen Township, and started where Academy Street and Bergen Avenue intersect.

It was the forerunner of Journal Square, and the beginning of our present town.

Chapter Five
A Hoboken Romance

Nemantha and Otsawa

Oratam:

The last account found concerning Oratam was the only negative piece of history involving him. The year was 1643, and Chief Oratam had to be in his late sixties. Three Dutch Patroons of Kiest had set up camp in the remaining back woods of Hoboken. They had "found" Oratam, and had given him a large quantity of Whiskey. These sadistic soldiers decided to taunt and ridicule the great chief. They spoke to him in abused English and demanded either a tax from him or "his leggings".

They challenged him to make good use of his bow and arrow while he was drunk. Oratam silently answered them by extracting a small arrow from his pouch and killing Van Vorst. He then asked the other two men, in perfect English, if he was "able" or not, and then disappeared into the forest.

Captain David Petersen De Vries

A Hoboken Romance

by M.A. O'Brien

1609 September 12 to October 4

September 12…The crewmen had spotted two natives in canoes and had alerted the captain. Hudson, dressed in his most decorated red ceremonial captain's suit, boarded a small boat, with first mate Robert Juet as scribe, and a few able sailors and came ashore.

On the shore, chiefs and wise men had formed a circle and were sitting cross legged on the beach. Several natives stood guard nearby, as Hudson with great pomp and ceremony, ordered a bottle of brandy from the ship.

The natives were amazed at the color of these newcomers skins, and their dress, especially the red man whose clothing glittered and sparkled like the sun, and whole hat was plumed with a giant feather.

They called him Manitto, (Godlike)

Hudson retaliated by pouring Brandy for the chiefs! Quizzically, each sniffed the strange liquid until one brave dared to drain the cup dry. Within minutes he had rolled on the ground and appeared to be dead, but soon awoke and demanded more "firewater!".

Soon all present were intoxicated and Hudson sent back to the ship for more presents for his new friends. He provided, "beads, axe heads, hoes and stockings, asked for land and promised to return.

When Hudson was preparing to pull up anchor, a native climbed aboard and stole a pillow. A crewman cut the native's hand off and pushed the body overboard where it sank out of sight. Two other curious natives were captured as slaves to be sold, and tied, but both escaped into the river via the portholes of the ship.

Hudson pulled up anchor and sailed upriver, putting as much distance as he could between his men and the overly curious savages. As the ship reached the tip of the Minna Atn (New York City) he found trouble.

A single canoe appeared, in which stood one of those who had escaped. It was followed by many other canoes of braves all brandishing bows and arrows.

Six muskets fired from the ship and three braves fell.

Suddenly the shoreline was alive with red men "about a hundred of them, all firing arrows." Cannon and musket fire killed another three, and this first land to sea battle ended with "the losse of nine indians".

Hudson immediately put out to sea in full sail, and it is said that the tribe of Delaware, even to this day, called New York City, "Manna Hattn," meaning the "Place of the Intoxication!"

Later sea captains learned to conserve the good brandy for their own use, and instead brought "Hogsheads of Beer for trade." No later trade was completed along the familiar Elk trading trails of the woodlands without "minnie pishbee", a small beer.

A Hoboken Romance

Nemantha and Otsawa

On the second day of October, 1609, Henry Hudson, on his return voyage downriver, brought his vessel to anchor off the Southeast corner of Hoboken, in four fathoms of water. He sent two of his men ashore, in a small boat for the purpose of trading with the Indians and procuring corn, tobacco and venison. The sachem chiefs, were already assembled in grand council fashion, to debate upon what the best course of action would be regarding the visit of the pale faces and their white winged canoe.

Some were for pursuing them to instant death, in revenge for the loss of the warriors, that had been shot by this vessel's crew on her previous upriver voyage, occurring several days before. The older chiefs and wise men advised caution, as they did not know how to deal with these strange people whose weapons flashed and roared with the anger of the Spirit of the Thundercloud.

The powwow was interrupted by several young warriors, who had observed a small boat being put off the vessel, and crewmen rowing ashore. Some of the tribe were ordered to assemble on the shore, as if to give the strangers a welcoming reception, and to invite them to land by various signs and gestures.

But treachery was soon made apparent, for the boatsmen had rowed to only within a few yards of the shore, when those in the boat were greeted with a shower of arrows that fell thick around them. This device wounded one rower in the shoulder, and the companion sitting adjacent to the wounded man, seized a musket and discharged it, thereby killing one of the natives on the shore.

The natives, decided that they may have too great a price for their temerity, and disappeared into the trees leaving the visitors to return to the anchored Half Moon in peace.

Hudson was very much offended of this treatment by the natives, but was yet in desperate need of supplies. He refused to take the advice of his mates, and to land with his whole crew to "chastise the Indians for their treachery."

Hudson considered that the wound of the injured man "was slight in nature", and that he had already been well revenged, and he also wished "to be more prudent to encourage a friendly feeling on the part of the natives for fear they might be overpowered by the force of their numbers and thus be utterly destroyed."

Moreover, they were "in want of fresh provisions and vegetables: and he was greatly afraid his men would suffer with the scurvy, during the long passage across the Atlantic on the upcoming voyage home.

It was therefore resolved shipboard, to "make another attempt to approach the shore, under a flag of truce, " but while the necessary preparations were being made for that purpose a seaman spotted a canoe, "being put off from the island," containing "two of the principal chiefs."

They were gingerly allowed to approach the ship, until Hudson became satisfied of their peacable intentions. Then they "were permitted to come on board, bringing with them "several otter skins, as presents."

The two chiefs apologized as well as they could for the rudeness and in-hospitality of their young braves, who they said had acted in opposition of the expressed wishes of their chief and expressed deep regret at the loss of one of their best braves.

This expression of friendship was well received on the part of Hudson, and he ceremoniously presented the chiefs "with a few beads and trinkets" and also consented to make them a visit that afternoon on shore.

The chiefs promised Hudson hospitable entertainment, and asked if he would witness an exhibition of ball playing, by the natives, as well as viewing and participating in the native welcoming dance and feast.

Hudson agreed and with utmost eagerness he awaited the coming afternoon, while a cadence of drumbeats from the trees announced the upcoming event.

Hudson, in great spirits, made his preparations. The warriors donned their finest buckskins and painted their faces, while the village maidens themselves assumed all of the arts, which the female sex of all nations,

Nemantha was the name chosen for her by the namegiver, as was custom. It was said in the village that the old chief was pleased, as he had been given many sons. It had been uncounted moons, since a daughter was born into the tribe. This was not usually an event for celebration, as the life of a squaw was worth little. Women were respected as beasts of burden, wood gatherers and child bearers and very little else. Occasionally a precious few would exhibit talent, in the beading and quilling of mocassins, and the designing of copper ornaments, usually patterned after their totems.

Their doeskin dresses reflected the most intricate and artistic designs and jewelry. It was these precious few talented individuals who were expected to teach their talents and arts to the rest of the tribe.

Trading was accomplished, for corn, at nearby Weehawken, with the peaceful Minsi speaking tribe, and snakes were gathered at Siskake (Secaucus) for occasional religious ceremonies. A rare visit by a trapper or surveyor would provide an endless source of fascination, with a trade of whatever modern invention he could provide.

It was said that the old chief had in his possession, a ship's bell, and had traded several reams of sewan shells (wampum) for it from a long forgotten passing voyager. It had amazed and mystified him, and at sunset, while the campfires were lit, and the food was being prepared, it could be heard tinkling its strange melody from the direction of his wikwam.

He rarely spoke of it or displayed it.

A hand held mirror and comb had also accompanied the trade, and these he had graciously given to the women of the tribe, who learned to his disgrace to incessantly fight and insult each other for the temporary possession of these odd treasures.

Thus, whenever a passing ship would bring a trader, or a trapper, the drum beats would accompany the event, and the entire tribe would turn out in curiosity.

Women were not invited to the trade, as this was considered men's work, but accomplished their uninvited curiosity by camouflaging themselves carefully in the nearest copse of trees, to watch.

If an especially interesting item captured their attention, they would keen and sing from the trees, with natural bird songs, and Owl's cries, and this became continued source of amazement to the trappers and traders, who usually sat in the circle with the chiefs on the beach.

Squaws would be punished if they were seen, with one exception. If a trader or a ship's captain or any member of the crew showed any sign of violence of behavior toward the chiefs, the entire tribe, men, women and children would suddenly appear, in front of the dense forest, standing silently in the colors of the sunset. Trades were held in the late afternoon for this reason, as dusk shadowed the shoreline, and the dense forest provided immeasurable cover.

This particular exercise in military strategy, was the cause of many a comment in early pioneer history. Sixteenth Century Dutchmen recorded statements that "there were no Indians in this area." Ship's logs read "hundreds of natives, previously invisible to the naked eye, were spotted among the trees."

Hudson's log and Pauw's Journal number "seven tribes in this valley" and eventually as trade increased in the valley bearing Hudson's name, natives were counted "in the thousands."

Nemantha

Nemantha was her namegivers name. It was the Lenape word for precious, and as she grew, the old chief saw to it that she was missing none of the arts of "the original people". As she grew to womanhood, no maiden of her nation was the possessor of such regal beauty as hers.

Much of the dormant child had left her, and her new flowering womanhood had blossomed, and her new form, straight as an arrow, was modeled on exquisite grace. This timeless beauty, which has existed throughout the ages, in song and legend and poetry, was given as hers. This is the beauty of mysterious womanhood which is so delightful to gaze upon, and becomes so utterly bewildering to the senses of men.

The low murmur of her voice was as delicious as dream music, her laugh like a bubbling bounding brook. Her tender step was as agile as a doe of the forest, and her keen brown eyes as sharp as eagles. Her demeanor was as mild as the doves, which she fed and befriended in the forest. Her light canoe was the swiftest on the rushing river waters, and the accuracy of her arrows was a certain and instantaneous death to the deer or the fox.

She was the unsung pride of the tribe, and the sole and precious joy of the old chief, her father.

Many a brave had cast a wistful glance in her direction, as they passed her in daily living, and many a decorated warrior had spoke in vain, to the chief, for her heart. The old chief knew that her imminent departure from his lodge would accompany her marriage, someday, bud had thus far refused to allow his lodge the loss of her, and had frowned on all suitors.

Nemantha was yet pure in thought and deed, and totally without guile, for her heart strings had never yet been plucked, with any other emotion than filial piety for her father. The sweetest mountain breeze of a summer morning had never visited it's scented perfume upon a more lovely woman than the old chief's daughter. She exhibited her presence and tribal dancing at all Lenape formal occasions and feasts, and much pleasured the tribe.

Just past the supper hour, at ship's bell, Hudson, resplendent and official, in his red captain's suit, and accompanied by several officers, and a few trusted crew members as rowers, left his vessel and was taken ashore.

The local chiefs and principal braves stood waiting patiently on the sand to receive him, and as thought to ascertain that their intentions were of peace, a considerable number of the tribe's women were allowed to make their appearance among the welcoming party.

Nemantha appeared, her soft doeskin dress qulled and decorated in the most becoming manner of the tribe. Her dainty feet were encased in matching moccasins of most exquisite workmanship, quaintly and carefully ornamented with beads and small shells, a visible tribute to the tribe's talent and handiwork.

Her leggings and deerskin garment were feathered with the tails of birds in various native profusion, and on her head she wore a t shaped copper crown, in which were set three small striped feathers of the gray eagle. She carried on her back, a thin quiver of arrows, and her hand rested on a bow, as delicate and in as perfect symmetry as herself.

Gingerly, she stepped through the standing crowd of curious Lenape women and children, and stood before Hudson and his scribe and crew, as a model of graceful dignity and tribal treasure.

Hudson gasped. He then remarked verbally and loudly, that he had never gazed on such queenly demeanor and beauty before, even admittedly among the stately blonde Holland amazonian dames of his own country women.

The chief was pleased at his reaction, and had some women bring food to the newly welcomed explorers.

Among the small retinue that landed ashore with Hudson was " a comely youth of pleasing presence", known to the crew as Master Carleton. It was spoken, in hushed tones on board, that he was a nobleman, and had shipped out of a spirit of adventure, having been "fairly well broken down in purse" by a "long course of dissipation and debauchery at home, in England", and was credited with " a naturally good disposition and a generous heart", by the crew. Carleton had mentioned, in passing that an evil feminine interest had led him astray, and had bid him to adventure on the high seas. From the excessive buoyancy of his spirits, and fondness for playful humor, he had made himself the favorite of his fellow passengers.

Reckless and feckless to the extreme, he was the first to climb the ship's mast, and whatever the danger, he was never deterred from even the most hazardous duty. No matter how fiercely blew the tempest storm, nor how turbulent the sea, he was always among the first and last on duty.

Fear never seemed to own a place in his seaman's bosom, and he placed his own safety worthy of not a thought, although his noble dress and appearance was in keeping with his station and character. He was always lightly yet most elegantly garbed, and in possession of all of the manly accomplishments of his era.

He spoke of his entries into society, amidst the fluttering hearts and fans of painted and gowned ladies, and the jealously and gallants of the men that accompanied such. It was gossiped that nothing could ever destroy his presence of mind, and that no fear of a personal duel had ever deterred him from laying siege to a lady's heart at court, even at the price of ruining her reputation. Such was Master Carleton, one of the choicest companions in seafaring adventure and company, of Henry Hudson.

When the small boat that contained the navigator and his companions touched the shore, they were received in the most courteous manner by the chiefs, and were, after a short beach powwow, eventually escorted to the well hidden village by "a hundred unarmed warriors." Here they "feasted upon venison and fruits" and "witnessed the sports which were gotten up for their entertainment".

Trade was fostered, presents were exchanged, and Hudson and his party were "constantly surprised at the unaffected cordiality of their reception."

No one was impressed as much as Master Carleton. Although bewildered by the scene, it seemed to him as though he were playing the part of an actor in a grand and wondrous romance. The wildness and beauty of the surrounding Hoboken countryside, the early Autumn foliage and the novelty of his situation had awakened in him his peculiar charms. His mind became enamored of adventure, and in his heart of hearts, he envied the free sons of the forest the very liberty they enjoyed, and half made up his mind to desert the ship and join them. He thereby relinquished all thoughts of home, and the many friends and enemies that he had left behind him in England.

As might be imagined, it did not take long for Master Carleton to discover and begin to admire the beautiful Nemantha.

As his flirtatious and experienced eye fell upon her, his body thrilled with the pleasurable emotion of possessing her completely. His overactive imagination pictured to himself the most perfect of happiness. He would sacrifice the world he knew and all he had, to enjoy a lifetime with such unsurpassed and unspoiled beauty, and natural simplicity of heart. With such ideas travelling in his mind, it is not strange to suppose that our adventurer soon found himself an opportunity of paying his addresses in person, to his tanned daughter of the woods, and he sought her in secret.

At first they were unable to understand each other's language, and their communication had to be carried on, principally by signs, though to new lovers, even though they cannot speak, there is a hidden language of love that has a thousand ways to express itself, more excruciating and elegant than mere words.

In an instant, as quickly as a thought among the native summer leaves, time stood still and they became lovers. Nemantha was especially pleased to look at her new lover. He was strangely tall and pale and handsome, most unlike the braves of her tribe, and his soft words of love fell silently on her hearing, as a murmur of a bubbling brook in a pleasant and verdant wood.

She could not interpret all of his words by their meaning, but she knew that what he said was sweet, and her beating heart felt a strange and hitherto unknown sensation. He looked so tenderly into her eyes, and pressed lightly against her. They left the camp together and spent hours just wandering in the bypaths. She laughingly pointed out to him the native names of plants and trees, and tried to explain to him the nature of the various creatures of the forest. He placed upon her finger a ring of lustrous value, and her eyes sparkled with infinite delight, as she frequently gazed upon it.

He looked into her eyes and raised his hand to her lips, and she innocently withdrew it, but her heart was so tremulous with mysterious and unknown pleasure that she let it linger passively in her grasp.

He began to cover her with warm and passionate kisses. They expressed their love in groves of oak, chestnut and ewe trees, and she gathered him branches of the spice woods, and created for him a bouquet of leaves. She sung to him in low and plaintive tones, songs of love of her native tongue, and he in turn sang to her of the ditties of ship's voyages, and olden wandering troubadours.

What a delightful and delicious dream did all this seem to Master Carleton. It was as if he had been transported by some magic to paradise, into a land and time of wondrous beauty. A place peoples by strange and wonderful citizens, enchanted by an Autumn palette of flame and orange and purple. Squirrels were gathering their winter store of nuts in the deep forest, and the ground was strewn with the brown coated chestnuts that came tapping down from the tall trees.

The new lovers, holding hands, walked under them.

Unmindful of either the track of time, or the passing of moments, and losing themselves in each other with no thoughts of the past, and taking no heed of the future, they came to a silent and retiring spot. It was margined on one side by the river, and at present known as Elysian Fields. Here, upon the trunk of a fallen tree, they exchanged a mutual worship of each other's hearts. What wonder if Master

Carleton imprinted his warmest kisses upon the waiting lips of his love. What magic as Nemantha accepted and encouraged his strange and wonderful touch.

OTSAWA

Numbered among the braves of the Lenape Nation, there was none more fierce or bold than the newly appointed sachem chieftain, Otsawa!

Dark and stocky he was, and as powerfully built as the great grizzly of the forest. The poles circling his dwelling were decorated with the scalps of his enemies. It was counted by the storytellers to be more than one hundred slain in battle.

He was fastest on the foot paths as a runner, and the flight of his arrows were unerring. In the chase he was always foremost, and in legend he became sachem by frequently providing game for the tribe with his myriad and well practiced hunting skills.

No one brave could compete with him in athletic sports, and he allowed no man's shadow to better him on the tracking trails. Yet, his dwelling was lonely without the presence of a permanent squaw.

He had for many moons marked the budding womanhood of Nemantha as his own, and thus had sent several worthy gifts to the old chief in hopes of wedding his daughter. The presents, no matter how extravagant by native standards were always returned. Nemantha would not listen to his carefully cultivated and practiced words of admiration, and had ignored his frequent advances.

He had spoken, according to custom, to her father formally, and the old chief had told him that he would not force his daughter to yield her charms to one she was not ready to love.

The heart of Otsawa beat with soreness, and he looked with blighting envy and jealous eye on any brave who deigned to speak with her. The other braves avoided him, cautiously, lest they incur his wrath. This gave him time and space to dream of Nemantha, and he made a sacred vow to Manitto that none other than himself would ever possess her. He had even made an appointment with the medicine man for a love totem, which he kept in the bottom of his shoulder quiver.

On the arrival of the pale faced strangers, he marked the attention paid Nemantha with the utmost interest and scowls. He watched carefully, the handsome pale faced Carleton, in particular and his heart became maddened with jealousy.

He resolved to watch them and when the walked in the village together he observed their every action.

His heart became as dark as the storm cloud, when he was called to council with the chiefs, and sat stonily for several hours at Powwow with Hudson and company in trade.

Otsawa dared not show impatience in the company of the other chieftains, but crouched cross legged, secretly brooding, until the old chief kicked sand on the campfire to signal the end of the powwow, and send Hudson back to the ship.

Otsawa cared nothing for the white man's papers, "buying land", or the trinkets or food that accompanied the trade. His preference was war. He sat resentful and brooding in his wikwam after the meeting, nurturing a vague feeling of uneasiness. Even the beauty of the midnight stars overhead failed to comfort him in his misery.

Sunrise had come this morning all too suddenly and from his dwelling he could see the morning cooking fires being lit at the village.

Nemantha's was not among them!

Arming himself with his finest and sharpest arrows, and favorite Tomahawk, he paced to the village to question some squaws as to the whereabouts of Nemantha.

He learned that she had left the main village, in the company of the white man named Carleton, and that the old chief, overtired from the previous powwow with Hudson, which had lasted many hours, was asleep.

Maddened with jealousy and hatred, Otsawa resolved to track them and with the wary silent step and the watchful eye of the mountain lynx, he stepped on many paths, until he eventually picked up their trail.

Nemantha and Carleton were yet entranced in the magic of Elysian Fields. They were so absorbed in each other, and their own bliss, that they heeded not the evil presence of danger.

Still clasped in amorous embraces remained the lovers.

The morning sunrise had pushed the gleaming golden circle higher in the sky and pink and silver clouds were covering the horizon. Giddy with their newfound rapture, the lovers had totally forgotten time, and were basking in a new world, a world of each other in which they had discovered their passions.

The atmosphere was balmy and the fragrances of the wood and the fall foliage added to the magic. The bird songs seemed to sing into the forest, filling it with supernatural music.

They again locked in an ecstatic embrace, and in doing so became oblivious to all else.

Chief Otsawa lay concealed on an overhanging branch in an adjoining thicket. His proud heart beat with the fiercest passion and rage. He had stalked them silently and carefully as a wolf in pursuit of its prey. His jaw and loins began to ache with a dreadful determination, fueled by a bloodlust!

Who could translate the bitter agony of his brave heart as he beheld his Nemantha in the arms of a stranger. He grew wild with envy at the listless languid form of she who had refused him. Then he heard her whisper an endearment to the strange white man!

Otsawa carefully took aim and let fly the poisoned shaft of his best and most finest arrow, and thus ended forever the crime of she he loved, and the life of him who he hated.

The deed was ended!

His heart throbbed with the most violent of emotion, and he drew one long breath, as the forest echoed with a deadly feminine shriek, and a low moan of agony.

Otsawa stood over them looking at the arrow!

It had pierced both of them!

Otsawa squatted over the inanimate Nemantha. Even in death, she appeared as a beautiful flower of the forest.

His eyes bright with the bloodlust of his deed, he sang the Lenape death chant!

It was vaguely interrupted by a moan. Carleton was still alive!

Otsawa added words to his death chant.

"You, you dog of a pale face!"

"You came across the big waters to plunder in the village of the red man. The spirits that howl around the eternal fires of the Manitto are waiting for you in the darkness that never dies."

"Die and rot, white man, and your bones will be destroyed by the beasts of the forest, and the birds of the air. You will whiten here in winter storms and bake in summer sun, and your spirit will never leave this cursed field."

"Die, white devil!"

In vain did Master Carleton raise his eyes imploringly. Thoughts of home and his friends crowded into his bewildered brain. A vision of his childhood and his mother stood before him, and the wholeness of his life passed in front of him like a moving panorama.

He moaned in a feeble voice, as the swarthy warrior bent over him. There was no mercy in Otsawa for the pale face. His features were distorted by the death passion, and as he stood he was the picture of demoniacal revenge. His ears were deaf to all appeals for mercy, and the hand that had never spared a foe in battle now brandished the Tomahawk.

It quivered for an instant in the uncertain air, then descended, loudly smashing through the brain of the rash and unfortunate Master Carleton.

The protracted absence of Master Carleton began to give serious cause of alarm to Hudson and his companions. Carleton was not aboard ship! Hudson feared that he might have been decoyed away and feared the worst. Inquiries were instituted throughout the village, and search parties were sent out into the nearby woods.

The day was drawing to a close and Hudson became anxious to return to his vessel and pull up anchor. Carleton would not be the first sailor to jump ship, and would not be the last.

The old chief had already made inquiries all over the village for his daughter and then it was remembered by the squaws that she had been seen in the company of the missing pale face, and that Otsawa was among the missing also.

One of the younger braves had remarked that he had seen Otsawa, fully armed, leave the village, and had watched him disappear into the wood. The fastest runners were now dispatched into the search…Suspicious glances were bent upon the strangers, and the old chief began to grow alarmed at the absence of his daughter. Hudson and his companions offered to help…

They returned to the ship and came back to the village fully armed with heavy broadswords, cutlasses and muskets. This added to the distrust and murmuring among the tribe. Hudson had wisely resolved that if there was imminent danger, that he and his party would make it back to the ship, and leave the unfortunate Master Carleton to his own fate!

Suspense and suspicion thickened the air and added to the suspense of the parties, and then, in a space of time, suddenly and inexplicably halted!

Otsawa had in a moment, rushed into their midst and stood bearing the lifeless body of Nemantha!

Wild cries of horror arose from the assembled crowd. The old chief burst into furious screaming and threw himself on the lifeless body of his daughter. The death song of the Lenape filled the air mixed with shrieks and keening. Squaws and warriors gathered around Otsawa as he related to them the crime that he had witnessed and the punishment that he had provided.

Ominous glances were visited upon the strangers. Hudson was aware of this and from the earliest gesticulations and speech of Otsawa, he knew that the death of the Indian maid was somehow connected to Carleton. He became immediately convinced that the safety of his party depended upon his immediate withdrawal. Hudson and his companions began to retreat towards the shore, using the utmost caution!

He had quietly walked with his party to within a few hundred feet of his landing, when the screaming savages, excited by the fierce declarations of Otsawa, broke forth.

Fifty armed warriors began running after them in pursuit. Arrows began to fly at the hardy adventurers, and Hudson, being well armed returned fire. He retained his usual remarkable coolness, and returned the assault with well directed fire, killing two of the natives and wounding several others.

A running battle was maintained for several yards, and the waiting ship, hearing the fracas, and assuming the worst prepared to set sail.

It had soon taken the entire party aboard and was billowing sail, which soon took them beyond the reach of their pursuers.

They cast into the wind, under full sail, until the following day. The following day, being stormy with tide, and the East North East wind Hudson was obliged to weigh anchor and wait out the coming storm.

By midmorning sentries on deck spotted several canoes putting off from shore. They had approached the vessel but Hudson kept the savages away by the threatening musketry of the mariners on deck.

There was a much heated discussion and controversy regarding the disappearance of Master Carleton, but just before nightfall his fate was made apparent.

Otsawa had paddled his canoe out into the midstream of the river, in full view of the ship, and was raising upon a pole, a reeking head and scalp, while chanting loudly the war song of the Mohican!

This act in finality, ended the conjecture of the whereabouts and fate of Master Carleton, proving his untimely death to the satisfaction of all on board.

The morning of the Fourth of October, being " a fine cleare day," Hudson pulled up anchor and began his final return homeward.

Later, in England, Hudson recounted his voyage at the local pub, and under the influence of a loose tongue wagged by his favorite Holland stout, he verbally admitted to the casualties of his last sea voyage. Several seamen had been penetrated with arrows, he said, and there were several burials at sea because of consumption, but his saddest memory was of his good friend and gentleman companion, Master Thomas Carleton, who "lost his head over an Indian girl."

EDITOR'S NOTE:

It was improper, by custom to bury a native girl with the rest of the tribe who had disgraced the village. It was spoken by storytellers that the old chief, broken hearted, took the body of his dead daughter by canoe, across the river and buried her on the tip of the Minna Hattn, that is now called New York City. On the ninth line down, on the second deed buying Manhattan from the Indians is the name of the disgrace of the burial place of Nemantha. The Dutch called it "Hoeren Hook" (Whores Corner). Otsawa was present at the signing of the deed and put his mark on it with the other chiefs. His name lived on for many moons with the story tellers for his fierce battles with and unyielding hatred of the white man.

Indians returning captives in a 1764 drawing by American artist Benjamin West. Many whites developed close ties to the Indians who captured them.

Captain Adrian Post

There is no character in Hoboken history that deserves more recognition than Captain David Pieterz DeVries. His name runs like a thread through the entire second half of the sixteenth century. He also had an assistant who was quite as heroic as himself, but was rarely mentioned, with the exception of the first few articles of the Hoboken Observer, the first newspaper of the Hudson Valley.

Stuyvesant's mistreatment of the Indians, taxation and lack of concern for their illnesses was legendary. DeVries had already left for Staten Island, and had brought most of the surviving natives with him to keep them safe from the greedy clutches of Stuyvesant's guards. The Weehawken and other natives however, remained, and refused to leave their land. They banded together with other local tribes in the area for safety, and held powwows with the settlers and arriving pilgrims. Trades were accomplished in this manner.

Six volunteers were hired by Stuyvesant to torment the local citizens, pilgrims and natives. They were to attack any locals, "and were not to go any further than the neighboring villages." If Kieft was the first satanic actor in the destruction of the natives, then Stuyvesant and his squad of volunteers carried it to an extreme. Phony deeds, excessive taxation and continued harrassment in courts, of any connected native business emerged. Targeted were natives, sympathizers, and the politically disfavored. Fines built up to five Guilders a day for the most minor infractions, and property was confiscated by Stuyvesant's warriors at will, when a citizen could not pay. Most could not. Quakers began to be harassed, publicly scourged, and continuously charged with minor infractions of the law. The Indians were defrauded of all of their belongings, including their leggings and blankets. A pay now or forfeit your life policy was put into effect by the six hirees of Stuyvesant, and cruelty was rampant. The Indians kidnapped a settler and demanded ransom. Stuyvesant ignored them, and the Indians declared war on the soldiers of Stuyvesant.

The Esopus War

Seven tribes, led by Oratam, went through the woods from the "big rock" at Weehawken, all through Hudson County and "kidnapped" a hundred settlers, and their families. The captives were taken into the interior of the woodlands, and distributed among the tribes, according to their talents and needs. Some were tortured to death, some were adopted and some simply disappeared, never to be heard from again. Woodlands were searched to no avail. Whole villages disappeared and relocated, to again become invisible. A bitter valley winter kept searches at a minimum.

A newly arrived Captain and his wife and five children were among them. Captain Adrian Post, the main contributor and minister of the New Bergen Church, and his colonist neighbors were taken. Captain Post's wife more than two years later was to give an account of life among the Indians. She claimed they were well treated and learned much of survival skills. The sons of Adrian and Clara Post, Franz and Adrian, and their twin daughters, Clara, and Gertruyed, spoke well of the "kidnapping," Four of the children thrived in the captivity of the Lenape, but Maria, born small and frail, did not survive the first harsh winter of her stay with the tribe. Captain Post missed his family, and was a frequent guest at powwows, which were constantly arranged for ransom. He was the first to be freed, and his stay of two months with the savages resulted in his learning the language and signs, and being honored by the Lenape as chosen to powwow with those in Colonial authority. He made consistent appointments with the town fathers, always in hopes of peace, and fasts and prayer services were conducted frequently for the safe return of those involved.

Captain Post, it is noted also performed twenty six marriages during this time period, and more numerous baptisms. Burials were accomplished by the frugal Quakers in simple pine caskets, with an occasional broken mast on a grave to mark a Captain of the Sea. Sea chests, with inlaid stars and brass pulls when not used as hope chests, were requisitioned as caskets. German immigrants began carving decorations into the wood. Ships in full sail became a vogue, and eventually, German and Irish immigrants turned to stone to mark the places of burial. Tombstones became longer and narrower and were frequently accompanied by a well carved angel or religious figure. Dates of birth and death, and sometimes epitaphs covered the stone monuments, occasionally with humorous limericks or poems.

The very poor fertilized the earth with their bones, without benefit of markers, and early epidemics of various sicknesses resulted in mass burials or areas of land set aside by governments and charitable organizations. . Potter's fields abounded, and the whole face of the funeral profession changed.

Arriving immigrants on myriad ships had tripled the population of Hoboken, nearly as fast as Stuyvesant had the taxes. Quakers were soon outnumbered by other Protestant denominations, and other Christian congregations. Each set of migrators brought their own customs and Hoboken became a blend of ethnic and religious diversity. Stuyvesant capitalized on these immigrants, making himself and his political cronies quite wealthy.

Two years of bargaining for the return of the settlers brought no results. Stuyvesant ignored the ransom messages from the Indians, with one exception. On April 12th 1656, he "ordered" a contribution from the local merchants for "the poor prisoners." The merchants paid up and no account was given as to where the guilders were used.

Another account names September 16th 1657 as a date to be remembered. A popular local native was found frozen to death on the shoreline. He had chosen this mode of suicide, and was found sitting, facing the sun, by some of the Dutch school children.

The council chiefs organized, and sent a ransom note to release "four or five Christian children" who were captured two years before. Stuyvesant refused, and offered to send a letter to Holland asking for financial assistance for the prisoners, publicly, while privately his squad of volunteers quelled any assistance or complaints from the locals.

Adrian Post, in touch with DeVries, and missing his wife and children, held Powwows for release of the prisoners, with the Chiefs, Oritam and Pennekeek. Two winters in the New Jersey woods resulted in many of the captured settlers dying. One hundred were taken, including forty women and children, and smallpox and disease were claiming many.

There were sixty captives left alive, living with various tribes. They were ransomed and returned through Captain Post's negotiations at Powles Hook, a few at a time, and always against the direction of Stuyvesant..

Captain Post's wife and four of his children had somehow miraculously survived, as well as a few of his neighbors, but were now directly attributing the tragic deaths of those involved to Stuyvesant.

Public opinion, and the local media branded Stuyvesant "a monstrous criminal", and complaints were sent to the new English government in charge. The Indians, yet invisible, were a disappearing nation. Smallpox was rampant.

Thus in June of 1664, Oratam of the Hackensack, Pacham and Perwim of Communipaw and Pavonia, and Tantaqua representing Bergen held a powwow to give New Jersey back to it's rightful ruler, the King of England. Starving, frequently displaced on reservations, and their numbers dwindling from smallpox and alcoholism, they agreed to the treaty for food and blankets and wages.

The English Lords now in charge, confiscated and reworded all Indian documents, and the culture, language, art and legend of the local natives was lost to time and antiquity. The "scriveners" (scribes) who drew most of the papers up, "lacked the Indian ear", and so were unable to apprehend the precise sound of the spoken words, and thus altered the history and place names of our area.i.e. Ack en shack ee became Hackensack, Hopockan became Hoboken, Minkakwa became Bayonne, etc.

Captain Post, his school teacher wife, and his four children were credited with building the first church in Bergen, and the name Post survived many decades in Hudson County, including being listed in the Daughters of the American Revolution, the Baptismal and wedding records of several nearby churches, and the census of many generations. A May 6th 1685 baptismal record of the First Church of Bergen lists Captain Adrian Post, Jr. and his wife Catharina Gerrits, baptizing their three children Annetie, Franz and Flytie.

Also in attendance as witnesses were the sisters of Captain Adrian Post, Senior. The twin girls, Clara and Gertruyed, none the worse for wear for their two years of Indian captivity, had both married and their grown sons, Nicholas, Fytie and Johannes Booth, and their grown daughters Rachel and Maria Kip brought a numerous assortment of grandchildren, and their respective partners.

Captain Post, Sr. was buried in the Old Bergen Cemetary behind the Church he loved so well. The Bayonne location now holds several large oil tanks and is owned by EXXON. A broken mast, the symbol of a Captain marked his remains. Other Captains were decorated with huge broken posts, another symbol of the sea, with one in Staten Island of a Mormon Captain buried alongside his six wives.

ORATAM
Senior Sagamore and Sachem of the Hackensack Indians

Josiah Koombs and Captain Finn

Josiah Koombs, in his late eighties, was one of early Hoboken's most colorful characters, as well as the official town historian. He lost a leg in the civil war, and returned to Hoboken to become a well decorated and respected veteran. His return heralded the new reconstruction and this town and its social and economic culture became his life.

Whenever the Hudson Observer, the prototype of our local newspapers, needed an educated opinion, or a story on the local motion or commotion, Josiah would be sought out, and his quotes and opinions would find their way into the local papers.

He prided himself on presenting historically accurate, factual accounts of local happenings, and for more than two decades, well into his nineties, he was sought out for excerpts concerning life in Hoboken, and the surrounding County achievements.

His favorite reminiscence concerned Elysian Fields, when as many as ten thousand spectators would watch the free local baseball games, which were sponsored by a combination of the city government and the local brewery establishments.

There were several teams, mostly made up of neighborhood citizens, and the winners always shared kegs of beer and hot dogs with the losing teams. Popcorn in the famous red and white folding cardboard containers was sold at the field, as well as lemon phospate refreshment.

The sport began with amateur baseball, and eventually melded into four semi-professional teams, who were always involved in play-offs. They were named the Atlantics, Mutuals, Gothams, and Eckfords, with the Gothams mostly taking the lead.

Ferryboats ran daily between Manhattan and Fort Lee, and brought additional spectators. The mighty Hudson, calmer than it had been in centuries, was a busy, industrious river and provided easy access and local transportation to the surrounding area.

Also travelling on the Hudson was the famous Alida Steam Special, with her upright walking beam. It was the only steamboat in the world which boasted a steam calliope, and was invented by the Stevens family.

Stevens, not to be outdone by steam or any other local inventors was consistently donating to his beloved Hoboken and its citizenry. The flute like music could be heard and enjoyed for more than two miles in good weather, and lilting pioneer melodies often whistled out daily reminders of "the new waterfront generation", more than one hundred years ago.

Sometimes the awesome "Yankee Doodle" blasted out of the pipes, much to the amusement of shore walkers, who were approaching Stevens Castle as they meandered on Elysian Fields. Stephen Foster tunes were the most frequently played, and Josiah Koombs and company, as most Hobokenites, was fond of whistling the familiar tunes. Most of them were composed here, via Stephen Foster, and the culture of the returning veterans connected with many of the songs and left a permanent peculiar influence on the music of the times. Whistling became the mode, and many songs that followed after that era had either whistlers blowing tunes, or quartets from the local barbers.

Most citizens knew the words as well as the melodies and music in many forms, was escalated and evolved from Hoboken.

The local taverns and bars were always full of music, and any new melody worth keeping passed inspection by whoever could perform. Josiah entertained frequently with his best barroom buddy, the son of the famous retired sea captain, Sir Simon Finn.

Sir Simon Finn was thought of as a bit of a character, and the natives gave him the name, "Steamboat Charley". No one could deny that Steamboat Charley was an important part and parcel of the aquatic and nautical history of the river faring Hoboken.

Steamboat Charley held another distinction, and his contribution to the local scene was considerable. He claimed to be the fourth generation Finn to be hired on the river to pilot seaworthy crafts. His particular decade as well as his fathers and grandfathers before him was a showcase of seaworthy talent.

His family's seaworthy contribution began with river rafts, and passed through the century on flat barges and steamboats. It was bragged that there wasn't a seaworthy craft on the river that Steamboat Charley or his family hadn't sailed.

Hundred of accredited unofficial Captains had made nautical voyages on and around the waterways of the mighty Hudson, and most were never given their place in history, but Steamboat Charley and his seagoing companions, sober or otherwise, inherited some of the fame.

Steamboat Charley remained memorable in the eye of the Hoboken public. Like most resilient Hoboken natives, he was in possession of more than one talent.

Besides piloting the Alida Steam Special on the river Hudson, and occasionally turning the ship's wheel over to the cabin boy to play the infamous calliope, he displayed another talent, which extended far beyond his seafaring capabilities.

He liked to sing Opera!

Early Hoboken culture was no stranger to the world of opera. Many citizens expressed an avid interest in the burlesque and bawdy river music, which was well publicized here, but there were always those who considered themselves, "of a higher nature", and who eagerly awaiting the coming Showboats for their peculiar form of entertainment.

Showboats arrived here from New York City, and ports in Europe, carrying the costumes, culture and arias of the world's most famous operas and operettas.

Jennie Lind sang here, and was often entertained by the city fathers upon her arrival with a brass band and the key to the city. Maria Theobald, the diva, from Germany, performed German opera most popularly, and was much admired as an entertainer.

Horse drawn carriages could be rented, to meet the shows and the H.P. Green Carriage Company, financed by the Stevens family, and outfitted with the finest and showiest velvet and tassels, taxied and transported the cultured gowns and tiaras, tails and top hats to the familiar operatic arias.

This provided whole columns of fashion statements in the Weekly Observer, and the gossip and the who's who of Hoboken graced the weekly news. Theater Programs were printed locally which also served to thrive the two new printing establishments in town, and added interest and fashion acumen to the budding lives of Hoboken citizens.

The skills of factory workers were exploited in the new economy, as ladies bloomers and men's pants factories opened. Zippers, invented here, had become the rage of fashion in Europe. The fame and invention of the zipper, which began in Hoboken, and had traveled all over the civilized world, had returned here, under the direction of Gideon Sundebach, a Swedish immigrant.

Hoboken's contribution to the fashion industry is yet another publicized first. While "bloomer" factories, manned by the newly arriving immigrant workers, abounded in several locations in downtown Hoboken, the fast moving new fashion industry was seeking a comfortable solution to ladies hook and eye corsets, and high buttoned shoes with complicated laces.

Inventor Whitcomb Judson designed a "clasp locker" for infant shoes in 1891. It was a simple device with a simpler principal. There was one row of hooks and eyes, neatly folding into another, topped by means of a tab. It was flawed and caught on everything, while inappropriately bursting open at inopportune and inconvenient times. Dubbed "the interlock", it stayed in the patent office for nearly twenty years.

In 1913, on the Twenty-ninth of April, a young Swedish immigrant from Hoboken redesigned it, by creating "smaller interlocks on more flexible material backing". He called his patent a "separable fastener" and it became useful on gentlemen's gloves and tobacco pouches.

Gideon Sundbach opened a zipper factory in Hoboken, and sought finance to expand. B.F. Goodrich sought out the invention and put it on galoshes and boots. Demonstrations to show the public the new fastener were given all over town.

A famous novelist and friend of Gideon Sundbach, while demonstrating the new invention, stated publicly, "Zip, it's open, Zip, it's closed!", which was picked up by the local newspapers.

The Zipper, as it came to be known, now had a title, but had not yet made it's full contribution to our society.

The U.S. Army decided to test the new invention on "flying suits". The tests were so grueling that the suits dissolved and disintegrated, but the zipper had outlasted the material.

In 1917, America entered the war, and the United States Navy ordered "zips" with the other branches of the service following suit.

England became fascinated with the product and displayed an oversized zipper at their Wembley Empire Expedition, inviting the public to try it for themselves. The "fastener" was zipped and unzipped three million times, by the public, without catching.

Paris and New York fashion houses adopted the new artifact, with men's trousers soon catching on to the craze. Two young Hebrew brothers, popular new icons of the garment districts of the world, the Levi's, decided to add a line of zippers to their strong buttoned western work "trousers", made of denim.

Thus, Hoboken's own Gideon Sundback earned a Doctorate in Invention, after making millionaires of all of his business partners as well as himself. He died in 1954, a famous and well respected inventor.

How Josiah earned his nickname

Mr. Koombs, a.k.a. Steamboat Charley was also fond of speaking frequently on unpublished scandals concerning local gossip. In particular there was the rivalry between steamboat inventors. Specifically, Robert Fulton, backed by a wealthy Livingstons who resided here, who owned and managed most of the river traffic, and the Stevens Family, who were relative newcomers from England.

The rivalry began shortly before the plans of the steamboat culture were translated into reality.

According to Josiah Koombs, Steamboat Charley, the rivalry began during one of the numerous and well attended Church Square Band Concerts, given by the city, for the musical and aesthetic entertainment of it's inhabitants.

Hoboken's river traffic became a beckoning entity to the invention and improvement of river vessels, thus bringing many new inventors to the shores and docks of the waiting and willing river culture. A few even achieved a certain notoriety in their respective fields.

Robert Fulton was a constant visitor here, in between trips to France and England. He was young, moderately wealthy, and extremely handsome, and attended the local music concerts frequently, until an incident turned the tide of public opinion against him.

It seems the young and handsome Fulton was "spoken to and challenged to a duel", for "making overtures to the very young and beautiful wife of aging Edwin Stevens, during a Church Square Band Concert.

When any media interview was conducted by the local press, concerning said subject matter, "general business competition" was always quoted as the reason for the Fulton-Stevens war on the river.

Steamboat Charley notwithstanding, via Josiah Koombs, spins a more scandalous version!

Mary Picton, daughter of a minister, was barely seventeen when she married aging Edwin Stevens in New York City in 1836. He was forty-one and had just come into his own as quite a successful inventor. It seemed Mary, the picture of propriety and high social standing, had accidentally dropped her dainty parasol into a small puddle on the concert field.

A very handsome and gallant Fulton, most appropriately attired as a gentleman in white gloves and top hat, retrieved said parasol, and flirtatiously presented it to the lovely lady. "I am sure your father would appreciate my returning your most lovely possession, " he was said to say, while adoringly kissing her hand.

Fulton, freshly returned from Paris and his roommate Benjamin Franklin, was enjoying some artistic notoriety in Hoboken for his art. His artistic endeavors consisted of hand painted miniatures on porcelain of royalty, and society's famous ladies and gentlemen. He had begun the vogue in England calling these treasures, "cameo paintings". The sale of these wonders was ever aided and abetted by his charming personality and attractive appearance.

The local media, much to the chagrin of Stevens followed Fulton everywhere for stories of interest. He became a dashing public figure in our history.

Stevens was doubly insulted, as he was already harboring a smoldering resentment and abiding hatred of Fulton. Stevens and his son Robert had already designed "the Phoenix" a better built and more lasting steam invention than Fultons, but it was not quite as ready for trial.

Fulton's steamboat came in first, and garnered all the local and national publicity concerning steam travel. The Stevens family, from this time forward had used all of their money and influence and political interference to break Fulton and his company down. Colonel Stevens and his sons would not enter into any competition on the Hudson until the Livingstons and the Fulton North River Steamboat Company were forced out of business in 1826.

Local scuttlebutt surrounded Robert Fulton, and some had branded him a coward. Stevens, after the band concert incident, had challenged Fulton to "his choice of weapons", for either a duel at dawn, or a sword fight. Stevens was adept and deadly at both, and his reputation with the sword and pistol was legendary.

Robert Fulton "refused the glove", and returned by ship to his Parisian apartment and his roommate Benjamin Franklin.

Always the artist, and never to be left without the last word, he composed a poem before he sailed on the tide, and had it printed full page, in all of the local papers.

> *Of all the causes which conspire to blind,*
> *man's erring judgement*
> *and misguide the mind*
> *what the weak head with*
> *strongest bias rules*
> *is pride...*
> *the never failing vice*
> *of fools"*
>
> *Robert Fulton*

The Parasol and the First Official Meeting

Steven's young wife's parasol had officiated a scandal, which also in another manner had entered into the first official council meeting of the new Hoboken.

It was held, for lack of proper space here, in Bowling Green, New York, on March 28, 1855.

It chartered the city of Hoboken as a township, and served to officially legitimize the Stevens Ferry Service. Both were already well in operation, as was Hoboken, but the city fathers felt that new rules and regulations should replace the old.

Charters and laws were gradually improving as the township grew, and it became necessary to legitimize everything in as an official capacity as possible.

The first ordinance introduced, legally was to outlaw ladies parasols! It was sponsored by the H.P. Green Carriage Company one of the township's major businesses, and backed up by several stable managers.

The ever vigilant town ladies, not yet having the power of the vote, quietly revolted at home, in the name of fashion and the ordinance was tabled so many times that it never passed.

Frightened horses yet bolted when those prototype umbrellas were flashed open, and stable managers still complained.

The newly appointed council ignored these complaints but did manage to pass "widening the pavement of several streets to provide carriage room." This opened a path also, for new words and designs of carriages to enter the nation's vocabulary by way of Hoboken.

Chaise, Caliche, Coupe, Cabriolet, Landaus and Phaetons pranced amidst the horses on the newly widened Hoboken pavements, and provided the culture and the prototype of the coming motorized automobile.

The "Footman's Coach" was the first to have "headlights", and the Phaeton and Cabriolet Coaches boasted of a "brake" that locked the wheels and kept the horses from bolting, while the carriages awaited their riders and drivers.

In this manner in the late 1800's, along with the improved inventions of the H.P. Green Carriage Company, and the last of the stable managers and their horses, some of our aquatic travel gave way to land transportation.

Previous town meetings, held in taverns and running back for a century now had an official capacity, and some of the history was written into the first town meeting as a symbol of how far Hoboken had come.

The first meeting makes mention of two.

The city fathers, action on complaints from the citizens had "ordered a local pig farmer to move his pigs outside the city limits, and offered to pay the moving expenses. He moved his "farm' to Secaucus.

Another article deputized the locals and organized the militia to "chase the Gypsies" out of the Fox Hill Forest area, as the farmers were missing chickens, and worried about their daughters being kidnapped.

It was recorded that the Gypsies did leave, but doubled back and set up camp in a hidden glade slightly West of Elysian Fields (now Park). Their fortune telling talents and roving lifestyle soon captured the imagination of the local citizenry and the Gypsies remained. Later meetings were fraught with "fines" leveled upon them for fortunetelling and chicken stealing. The local media, never short for a story in our new growing Hoboken, dispatched an artist from "Hudson's News Magazine (Gleason's Pictorial) to their camp, and the following article and artist's hand drawn rendition of their campground appeared in the local paper.

"Our artist has sketched for us a scene which represents the gipsies as they appear in Hoboken, New Jersey. They are encamped a little West of Elysian Fields, and their arrangements are as simple as Western Indians- a small tent, constructed of hoops, with the ends stuck in the ground and canvas covered over them. They travel from place to place in a covered wagon, and upon arriving at a suitable spot-which is such a one as they are most likely to find custom by telling fortunes- the small tent is struck and a fire built by which they cook their meals and await the arrival of such persons as are disirous of a peep into futurity."

"These gipsies consider themselves of Egyptian descent, and preserve among themselves their own language, and have their own King and Queen, and adhere to rules and regulations laid down by them. They are still to be found in tribes, scattered throughout Europe, living a roving life, continually moving from one place to another. There are seven (tents) in all of these at Hoboken, and they are only remaining here to receive the rest of their tribe, whom they expect to arrive in this country to rejoin them; they have expressed a strong repugnance to living as civilized people do; and when told that in time they must find a more hospitable and honorable employment, and be enabled to live in a more comfortable manner, they express no desire for such. At present they are exciting much interest in Hoboken, and many go over from New York to see them daily, and to get from them a supposed knowledge of futurity."

Fortune telling, scrying, crystal ball reading, and card reading became a rage for a decade, until the residents began to complain at council that they were being defrauded…and the "gipsies from Hoboken" moved on to more greener pastures.

Their departure was encouraged by the city fathers decision to make a few designations of proper land sections as PARKS…and we begat Elysian Park, Church Square Park, and Steven's Park. Eventually Columbus Park was also added, replete with appropriate sculpture, statues and monuments of the times. The current administration under Mayor Anthony Russo has added, along with shipyard development Frank Sinatra Park and several small parks and walkways along the river.

Another, altogether new Hoboken has emerged adjacent to the mighty Hudson, and the city fathers of old, and the natives of old, long gone, would be amazed and mystified at the progress of this prarie township which has now become a city.

It no longer basks in the shadow of New York City, but has with careful planning come into it's own in the new millennial time, in which we gratefully reside.

Hail Hoboken, long may you reign in the hearts and minds of the people who love you!

M.A. O'Brien

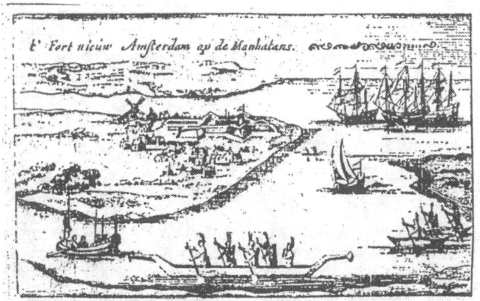

Oldest known view of the North Jersey shore front, about 1626. In the distance can be seen New Amsterdam. The soil of Pavonia, from Castle Point to Constabel Hook is shown in this picture. Powles Hook is at the lower left corner.

Sloops and Whales and
Nautical Tales

The seafaring Dutch held to their oceanic culture and as soon as they landed began the plans for shipbuilding. Oversized yachts that originally carried the settlers here proved to be too clumsy for our narrow rivers and inlets. Every coastline in the world had learned to build ships, and some were more seaworthy and lasting than others.

Our Hoboken which was then documented as Mauritania, on the River Mauritanius, was no exception. The main financier of the first few voyages here was the Prince of Orange, Maurice, by name, and the Dutch Masters wanted Hoboken to be called Mauritania of the New World. Maurice and his money were to be so honored,, but eventually, Maurice and his money went up in smoke, and the Indian peacepipe name prevailed. Hoboken, however you choose to pronounce it or spell it or corrupt it will always be Hoboken.

Maps, charts, and official charter papers all have names that have since been corrupted by language and custom into other names. Ahasimus was to be Jersey City. In order to simplify the area, and perhaps as an insult to the dependence of pioneer life upon the Dutch Masters, the settlers and Quakers decided to keep the Indian names, as many of our towns and rivers attest. (see Touching Leaves Woman)

The river became the next frontier of culture and invention.
Thus, necessity became the mother of invention, and a simpler, more compact craft evolved into our river culture. It was credited with a huge mainsail, and had the most immense sails of any vessel that was designated as a craft on the river.

These slightly less than seaworthy experiments were faulted with nautical problems. They needed to be constantly manipulated against the winds and the rolling salty tides, and they had heavy canvas sails that the sea rotted and tore.

Sailmakers were in high demand, and canvas was measured and sold as precious cargo.

Docks were immediately designed to sequester these marvels, and the design of the seventy foot crafts and the testing became known in the new culture as "the Hudson River Sloop".

Pantalooned Dutch, puffing always on their long pipes of tobacco planned and built and sailed and raced these prizes. Arguments over whose was more "wide bottomed" added new expressions and descriptions to the sea lingo and became a permanent part and parcel of the present pioneer culture. Expressions like "billowing the mainsail", "taking to the canvas", and "in the drink", became popular and added interest and perhaps a glass of stout and a bet to the races.

It was great entertainment and it was common to view more than fifty sloops out on "the Witches Tide". Wives complained that their "Knickerbockers were drunken" and there was many a brawl on land after a sail!

The watercourse, lacking the circular pattern of a common earthly landlubber racetrack was planned past the Cave of Echoes, later to be known as Sybil's Cave, and stretched aquatically all the way out to a jutting sand bank, named "Sir Anthony's Nose." This was a tribute to the first Knickerbocker who had the distinction of winning the first official race.

He had proudly named his hand crafted prize, and best attempt of a sloop after himself. His "ship" was known to the locals as "The Anthony", and was outfitted and appropriately painted "in the Italian Style" complete with "hand painted grapes " across the 'bough.

Grapes had somehow always materialized in the design and fabric of Hoboken, even to later centuries in art and architecture.

Anthony Van Twaeller (Twiller) displayed another distinction of which he was also as proud. He had an enormous proboscis, (nose) modeled in the style of Cyrano De Bergerac.

It seemed he was becoming a close second in the first official race and the cheering Dutch from the shore were screaming in their gutteral language for him to win.

One of the other sloops, by a providential puff of wind, had accidentally cut his opponent off, allowing Van Twaeller to glide into first place. It was counted that fateful day, that he "won by a nose", and for many years the finish line was fatefully and appropriately dubbed "Anthony's Nose". It later was renamed several times, and the millennial fisher folk of today call it Ambrose Lighthouse.

These Knickerbockers, named by the other pioneers by the peculiar leggings that they wore, kept their shipbuilding talents and their knickers in place, and dry, along with their sense of humor.

For a small space of time, they coexisted peacefully with the natives and other pioneers. These sloops were the first and original water taxis and became the transport of the Hudson up and down river for decades. Although the sloops marked a nautical place in the history of Hoboken, they were very soon to be replaced by a more modern invention.

Steam had been discovered as a form of energy, and the steam-boat, paddled or not paddled, was soon to hiss it's noisy way into our aquatic history.

River travel of all sorts of vessels opened up the entire seacoast for strange and exciting contraband. Chinese artifacts were in great demand, and enthralled our early inhabitants with strange and wonderful cargo from faraway lands. Tales of piracy on the high seas, cannibalism and shipwrecks accompanied the returning vessels, and the music and poetry and writings of the time reflected "Colonial" America. The age of discovery had opened up the oceans of the world!

Docks were built and repaired continuously to await the incoming tides of commerce, and the ever increasing population of immigrants filled our Hoboken with settlers of all countries.

Sadness also traveled on the tides, and a very select few of the Dutch Masters engaged in the beginning of slavery. This incensed the Quaker Captains who would have nothing to do with this part of history. It however continued under cover of darkness!

The age of the article also enhanced candlemakers and their craft. The Dutch had brought this talent with them as part of their culture at home, but the new "Chinese Candles" each encased in their own ginger jar bowl, became the rage of fashion and decoration for each pioneer home. Filled with wax and lit, or whale oil and lighted, these became the prototypes of our modern Ginger Jar Lamps.

The docks became bazaars, and it was not unusual in the course of a day to see pigtailed orientals haggling in broken Dutch, peddlers of all nationalities who could sail, Sea chests full of wondrous articles, politicians and pirates dining together on the dock, and other assorted contraband laid out in public view for sale.

Arriving ships were greeted with great fanfare by the city fathers, and in this manner and mode of living, trade and commerce increased beyond our valley to lands far and near.

It was the age of the "gadget" and every new artifact was examined and if found useful, became part and parcel of the pioneer home.

Oddly, one popular hero took one of the new Chinese inventions a little too seriously, and was fined twenty guilders and given a suspended sentence for his participation in his only documented crime.

One of the first returning ship's had brought back firecrackers. Local hero and Indian activist Captain DeVries decided to test out this new invention on the shores of Hoboken. He took two of the natives with him, as was his custom, waited till the town crier had announced that all was well and had retired for the evening.

It was a quiet and peaceful star lit night on the shore of Hoboken, "ten of the clocke". The whistling rockets, exploding cherry bombs, and colorful eruptions in the night sky caused a panic here.

Local merchants and their wives and families, already in their night clothes and asleep over their stores and farms, assumed that the coast of Hoboken had been attacked by Pirates. They began to run through the streets in a frenzied panic.

Within a week, the Dutch Masters, already jealous of DeVries and his popularity with the remaining Indians, made a public issue of this panic and arrested him.

Accordingly, DeVries was fined "twenty guilders", and the trial provided much entertainment for the townspeople. The trial was intended by the Dutch Masters to portray DeVries as a nuisance and a detriment to Colonial life, but somehow it only served to increase his popularity with the majority of the populace.

Hoboken, via China, may very well have been the home of the first firecracker display in "the New World."

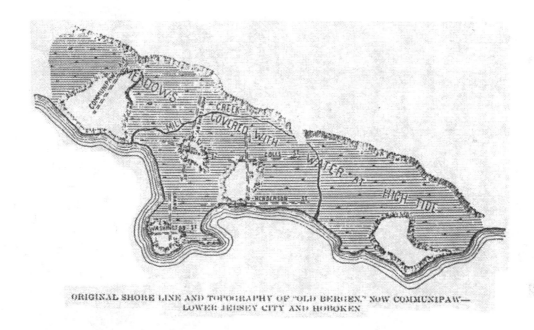

ORIGINAL SHORE LINE AND TOPOGRAPHY OF "OLD BERGEN," NOW COMMUNIPAW—
LOWER JERSEY CITY AND HOBOKEN

1674 Winfield Map showing most of our area at Witches Tide.
Note many sections of Hoboken were then part of the river.....

The Unnamed Civil War Captain

She sat on the train to Hoboken in her dark widow's weeds, her raven hair and eyes somber quotation marks escalating the already present aura of widowhood surrounding her like a silent shroud. Closing the boxcar window had drowned out some of the station noises, and her attention was immediately drawn to the children.

A small shy girl of three, a miniature of herself, stood quietly, refusing a seat, next to her mother, draping a tiny porcelain hand over her mother's arm. A younger child, a boy of three years, sat gingerly on her lap, fingering the clever stitches on his hand crocheted sweater.

A strident white whistle clouded the landscape and puffed noisily out of the engine car ahead, and startled all on board. This reaction by the young widow and her family captured the complete attention of a well dressed gentleman in passing.

His dove gray suit, spotless white gloves and top heat of the finest match identified him instantaneously as a wealthy member of the new gentry of the devastated South. He stared boldly at the beautiful woman before him. But Mary's eyes were riveted on the sweater of her son. She recalled, in memory, the pleasure that she had had crocheting it.

The kitchen slaves, back at the plantation had hand spun the yarn and presented it to her for the child's last birthday, not six months past. The white soft cotton had been dyed an appropriate shade of baby blue. It was deliberately constructed slightly too large, but was savored and shown proudly to grandmama, then careful folded into the hope chest in the massive colonial bedroom of the plantation.

Oh, the master bedroom, so provincial and baroque and huge. It was as massive as the master who owned it. The finest of silks and satins had always covered the giant bed and windows. So huge and now without him to share it! Muscoe? Typhoid had taken here dear Muscoe, one of the most proud and avid supporters of the Confederacy. A Congressman, if not loved by many at least respected by most! Typhoid had ruined everything, and what the typhoid hadn't taken, the war certainly had! Insufferable shortages of everything!

The child on her lap whimpered, and she kissed him on his little blond head, and adjusted his position so they could both look out of the window of the train. He was temporarily calmed as they both watched the passing unfamiliar sights of the busy new budding towns. Building was everywhere!

As her children were distracted by the passing scenes, her mind again returned to the plantation. Nestled on the summit of a grassy hillock, it was considered an epitome of everything Southern.

"Elmwood House of Virginia," Mary thought proudly.

Her residence, her home! Even just thinking the name out loud evoked waves of homesickness, and misted her lovely dark eyes, so deeply that one gentle tear rolled down her cheek and fell on the face of the baby.

"Mary!"

"Don't you recognize your own Cousin, Mary?!?"
"We played as children in your father's backyard in Princeton!"
The well dressed gentleman spoke further.

"Those were certainly happier times," Mary, "and I must say that your company made my childhood quite pleasant!"

He took a solid gold pocketwatch on a chain out of his silken lined pocket and opened the case to check the time! The gilded circular cover was intricately carved with a steam locomotive!

"May I inquire as to the health of your dear father?" "It was his recommendation that assisted in the obtainment of my first employment!"

" I am a banker, now Mary, and modestly wealthy if I do say so myself," he laughed. "The war between our states has done that to some of us," He was bragging..

Mary was trying to remember his name... Cornelius! Oh, yes, she thought ..Cornelius Whipple, a distant cousin on my father's side. Even as a child, he was a bragger, and Mary remembered him as being particularly annoying and obnoxious.

"I am returning to my father at this time, MR. Whipple, from my home in the deep South!", Mary said coldly, "I will certainly give him your regards!"

Sensing her aloofness, Cornelius suddenly felt less inquisitive and friendly. The child on her lap let out a plaintive wail. The little girl just sat quietly overdressed in her travelling clothes, and avoided his eyes.

"Please, it is a long trip to Hoboken", quipped Cornelius, "Allow me to purchase something to amuse the children!" "Absolutely not!", "that will neither be necessary nor welcome!" stated Mary flatly, but neither the coldness of her attitude nor her conversation was heard. Her answer to him was only heard by the clicking of the wheels of the train, and only served to punctuate the empty air. He was gone!

Mary was first elated, then saddened as her mind slipped back to the reverie of her past home and hearth.

The words and melodies of the sweet spiritual hymns of the slaves carried on the clicking wheels of the train, in cadence. How they sang after they lowered the casket into the warm brown resting earth! His casket, carved from the oldest tree on the plantation… His earth! All gone…probably appropriated and burned by the Yankee soldiers who had freed her!

Another gentle tear ran down her cheek, and she produced the finest lace handkerchief and dabbed at it sweetly.

She had been extremely fortunate to escape in time, and now fate had decreed that she and her children were safe on this train…talking to this …Carpetbagger! Anger welled up inside her chest, and lost itself in another flashback of life at the plantation.

"Miz Garnet, Miz Garnet, the Yankees is comin' up the hill" The house slaves were visibly panicking and screaming. One of her husband's prized pistols in each hand, she greeted a small handful of soldiers at the very door of her plantation.

Fear of her children's safety had caused her to stand her ground on the porch, in the rough breeze of Autumn, her black hair and eyes blazing with Southern womanhood.

"What do you want here, there are no men to kill!" she shrilled at them. "Only myself, an old woman a few slaves and my children!" She was frightened but somehow it didn't show, and she stood on the porch, hands shaking slightly, her eyes wide with fear, yet holding tightly to both pistols…

She then recognized the officer in command as being that of Albert Dodd, her stepmother, Martha's brother.

Of course, how very like her father. Her father, safe and conducting business as usual from his castle in Hoboken, had written of his concern for her safety, and the safety of his grandchildren, and had sent the cavalry!

Officer Dodd, apparently in charge, spoke crisply, as he dismounted a black and sweating horse. His troops remained mounted.

"I have come for you, Mary!" He approached her on the porch, ignoring the pistols, and pulled a theater program out of his Federally starched uniform, and held it out to her to view at arm's length.

She could see the hand written calligraphic script across the center of the flier.

Pass Mrs. Garnett, two children and a nurse was all it said. It was signed Abraham Lincoln.

Father had intervened with his usual business sense!

"It has become both dangerous and unnecessary to continue your residence here, Mrs. Garnett, and your father has sent me to fetch you!" "Please, time is of the essence, Mrs. Garnett, gather your children quickly, and be advised that there is a company of soldiers, not to our liking, less than an hour's march from this plantation."

"I cannot guarantee your safety and the safety of your children, should they arrive here unexpectedly." His words were punctuated by the sound of a cannon firing, and the distinctive firing of muskets not far enough away.

Mary's namesake, little Mary, who was held fast on the porch in the arms of a pregnant negro nurse, broke free and ran screaming in terror across the porch, and hid in the folds of her mother's dark silken gown. Some of the horses flinched in fear at the sound of the muskets.

Mary just stared! It was all too much to comprehend.

"Must I remind you to be quick, Madam?!" Captain Dodd spoke coldly.

"I cannot leave my mother in law unattended, Captain" said Mary quietly. The Captain admired her cool courage in this situation.

"Madam, your father has made previous arrangements to secure your Mother in Law to Charleston in safety, and that is the principal reason why her presence is missing here."

"If you and your children and your nurse are not ready to leave in two minutes, we will physically carry you bodily as prisoners of War."

While the Sunday touring Surrey was made ready by the slaves, Mary packed a small hand trunk, a shawl, some of Mary and Mercer's clothing, her elegant silver brush and comb set from her elegant dressing table, and a silver goblet with matching swans gracing it that Dear Muscoe had given her to donate to the church for communion.

These were her best and most useful treasures! The sentiment of these objects was the priceless part, the gold and the silver simply ornamental... The comb and brush set had been her very first anniversary present and was presented to her in full view of the annual ball at the plantation. How the Lords and Ladies had danced and how they had feasted that day.

A waiting soldier took the trunk roughly away from her and closed the lid!

Dear Musco Garnett, his gilt framed portrait was hanging in the main hall and looked down at her as she was descending the red carpeted stairwell. Muscoe!

Perhaps she could request the soldiers to take the portrait down! Another volley of musket shots tore through her thoughts! They were decidedly nearer and echoed violently across the plantation!

78

Two officers, awaiting her exit from her bedroom, relieved the other soldier of the trunk, and she in descending noticed that the children were already carefully dressed for travel by the nurse, and were already awaiting her presence in the surrey.

Bessie, the faithful slave nurse, quiet and calm in most situations, and a treasure herself, had dressed both children warmly and was sitting in the surrey between them. "One blessing at least, " thought Mary, "they were all too frightened to cry!"

Captain Dodd mounted with the three other soldiers, and waved his hand in a forward motion. At the signal from this officer in charge, a wild and bumpy gallop began. It lasted two bone jarring miles to the nearby Rappahonnack River bed.

The children had clung to her tightly all the way through the well camouflaged Virginia landscape! Muscoe had planted many of those trees, and they now, in providence provided needed cover.

A deep smoky mist covered this sad caravan as they finally broke through the woods and approached the shore of the river just before dawn!

"Diiiiisssmount!"

Captain Dodd had dismounted his troops and all stood sock still on the riverbank, waiting! Quietly as a still life painting, they waited in silence, shrouded in the silvery mist, as the first few strong rays of the morning sun opened the Southern sky.

A long strange, ghostly gray object broke through the shore at the river's edge.

Nearly invisible in the morning mist, the Southern Sun's first rays rose on a tiny shawled woman, soldiers carrying two blanketed bundled and a trunk, and a negress toting a smaller trunk, all being quietly rushed into this hissing contraption.

Several of the horses had reared in fear, and pawed the ground noisily, which had caused two of the soldiers to dismount and hold the reins, speaking soft words to the disquieted animals.

A stocky man in a dark sailor's garb seemed to be standing on the water in the eerie mist of the morning.

"You make too fine of a target, Captain!" laughed Captain Dodd.

"No worry, you Johnny Rebs couldn't hit the broad side of a barn!" the Sea Captain quipped back.

Almost comically, and with the utmost in perfect timing two musket shots sang over the bow.

"Cast Off!" shouted the Sea Captain, as Captain Dodd jumped to his horse. His companions mounted and the sound of hoofbeats could be heard pounding in the opposite direction, as a decoy. The ghostly tub had already glided away quietly to the silent sunken somewhere from whence it came.

"How comical, and how like a dream!" thought Mary. " How like father and his inventions!" "How far removed from this noisy clicking train, and this journey to the East!"

The tall overly friendly man was back. He stood over them offering the children small sacks of candy, individually wrapped in strange colorful paper.

The children were amused, took it suspiciously, played with it awhile, and unwrapped it. They became bored with it and threw it on the floor.

"How ungrateful!" thought Cornelius. "I was just beginning to make some headway with this very attractive widow." His thoughts on the subject became immediately transparent by the look of abject horror on his face.

Mary, carefully reading his thoughts, spoke up candidly!

"Cousin," she said coldly, but firmly, "My children have never seen Eastern candy, they don't know what it is!" "Nor have they ever partaken of white lump sugar, or any other of your Eastern accoutrements!"

Speechless at last, and feeling most unwelcome, Cornelius bowed slightly, and departed the car. The train, accustomed to keeping the secrets of it's many passengers, clicked on noisily, en route to Papa Steven's Castle in the East.

The Naugatuck Submersible

The First Submarine

The Naugatuck had been invented and built by the Stevens Family of Hoboken. It boasted of an unheard of ballast system, which could sink the ship slightly over three feet, in theory, assuring her a much smaller target for the inaccurate guns of the day.

Running with decks nearly awash, a steel gray, and only the top mast visible, the Naugatuck led four Navy ships into battle against the famous "Merrimack", and was later sent to New York City to guard against Confederate raider vessels.

The Ironclad Naugatuck was a highly unusual ship, far ahead of it's time, and proved to be a successful prototype for generations of new and innovative nautical ideas. Her unique features, water ballast system, rotating gun coil springs, twin screw propeller and armor platings were later refined and applied to modern warships in our time.

The adopted safety standards of the day, and the air tight fire room are still in use by the United States Navy and have saved countless lives. It is ironic that father and inventor Edwin Stevens had donated the Naugatuck to the war effort of the Revenue Marine Service (Merchant Marine) and that his patriotic generosity also served to spare the lives of his own daughter and grandchildren.

Mary and her children, Mercer and little Mary lived at Castle Stevens to wait out the war! She took a temper tantrum on arrival, which became part of the local lore of legend. The Stevens family was flying the Eastern Colonial thirteen star flag of from the Castle Gatehouse. She asked, as a Southerner that it be taken down, as it was an insult to the South. The Colonel flatly refused!

"The 'Naugatuck' was in commission for several months, and did good service in combats with batteries on the James River until the bursting of her 100-pound Parrott gun (without injury to her crew, who were below the armored deck) caused her retirement, and her place was soon supplied by the 'monitors' built in great numbers at that time.

"Experiments made on January 11, 1862, showed that a 10-inch gun could be

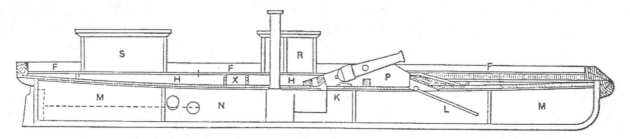

The 'Naugatuck'

loaded with charges of 11 pounds of powder and a ball of 124 pounds, and discharged four times in 139 consecutive seconds, the quickest time for a loading and discharge being 25 seconds."

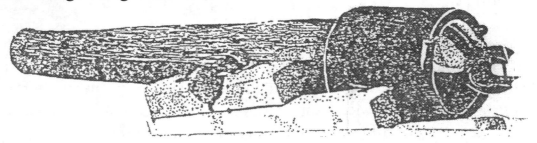

Editor's Note:

Mary married a second time... June 1, 1869 to Colonel Edward Parke Custis Lewis, Confederate States Army of Virginia...He was a grandson of Martha and George Washington

The Ghost Ship of Hoboken

by M.A. O'Brien

I beheld a hallowing and haunting tale of chivalry and generosity of times and days long gone..of Blues and Grays and slavin' ways and Castle Stevens goings on.

I tell the tale of a Southern Belle, one of Dixie's finest daughters, and how a ghostly ship from Hoboken spared her life in enemies waters..

It was transport for her children to the Castle Steven's fair, by the connivance of her father did she dwell in safety there.

Parental love can triumph throughout war and politic strife and love can sail it's children home, to equip a millennium later, the word stuffing of this tome.

A brave young mother softly sailed, through war torn seas I'm thinkin' first love secured a safety pass, and signed it Abraham Lincoln;

The Naugatuck, a battleship, was Stevens war donation, built in a cove in Hoboken commissioned in the East. Who knew that the misty morning fog, on the Rappohonick would conceal the progeny Stevens in the belly of the beast. and that a lovely Southern Belle with the gentle name of Mary would come to leave her home, heartbroken and survive to view the "new" stars and stripes from a Castle in Hoboken.

Who can know the bittersweet heartache and the gist of the true story? As the Serpentine Castle gate house displayed the new "Old Glory". Well traveled were here children, o'er land and war torn sea, both products of the winning North and the proud Confederacy…

Chapter Six

Touching Leaves Woman

The Story of Nora Thompson Dean

It was the way of the people to hide pain. Even the grandmothers and grandfathers would walk far away from the main tribe to sing their death chants, and wait, ultimately for the inevitable.

Deep in the Eastern woodland, away from the tribal conical huts, knelt a young squaw in the final stages of labor.

The smoky scents of Autumn penetrated the deepening dusk, as crisp fall leaves in myriad shades of red and gold and brown whispered down to the glowing frosted ground cover. The clear pre-winter air held a decided chill. Silently and semi-kneeling, in the way of the people, the squaw gave a long awaited final push.

The new mother gazed in rapt adoration at her perfect little daughter. Tiny and brown she was, and perfect! There was something strangely womanly about the child, and her infant fingers were strangely wiggling as if she were playing with them, or perhaps weaving.

The mother, elated that this one looked strong enough to live, laughed out loud!

Tall Feather, the name giver, stood quietly nearby in a copse of trees. She had long ago been entitled as the name giver of the tribe, and her intelligent brown eyes had taken in every detail of this particular birth.

"She shall be called Touching Leaves Woman," Tall Feather prophesied.
"Her words will be shared by many, and her honor will be much."
"She shall be a keeper of the people".
"She will be a gatherer and will share her talents and her totems with many tribes of the people and not of the people".

These were the words of the birthing in the old ways.

The ancient teachings and ways were fast disappearing at "Indian Mills Reservation". Hunters and warriors were spoken of no more. There was nothing left to hunt, and no war to fight! The entire culture, music, festival and art of the tribe depended upon these things.

Many feather prayer sticks decorated far too many graves, and the only music allowed on the reservation was the death song in the wind of a disappearing nation. Yet there were few who thrived in the hardship setting of reservation life.

Touching Leaves Woman attended a mission school on the reservation, and her name was changed, by her white captors to Nora Thompson.

Over time, she became a Christian. Through several generations, although married to a white soldier named Dean, she managed to keep alive the customs, music and legends of the Lenape.

She spoke and taught Unami (Hoboken Lenape) and became over the years a virtual repository of tribal learning. She was permitted to open a store on the reservation, featuring hand made native crafts by the tribes-people who still could make them. It was at first an attempt to raise funds for the reservation children, and also provided her with a small livelihood.

She was soon recognized as an Elder of her tribe, and was also given the honor of NAMEGIVER. She was admired by scholars, honored by Governors of Oklahoma and New Jersey, and decorated by Chiefs of many nations, including presidents for her gracious and patient teaching of tribal lore to children. She preserved the language of the Lenape for all time.

SOME OF THE LENAPE LANGUAGE SAVED BY TOUCHING LEAVES

land ock….meadow…asqu…swamp…assisku,,,pong….paug….river…sipo
bread…pone…corn…hosequen…meat…iwse…grapes…virum…
fish…lamiss…salt…secca
coast…aquewan…leggings…cocoon…shoes…mocassins…
tobacco pipe…Hopokan…snow…whinne (also the word for beautiful)
minna atn Manhattan, the Island of Hills
a dwelling wik…
warm……..wam
a valley Passaic elk Wapiti, Duck, Quink Quink, canoe…maholo…

water …ipis ipe

Woodland natives reckoned their time by moons. Each full moon made a month. One walk was about an hours travel, and one sleep an overnight trip.

Months were given specialized names by geographical titles…
March was the Green or Spring Moon.
April the Moon of Plants
May the Moon of Flowers
June was always called the Moon of Cherries Ripening,
July was the Deer and Game Moon
August the Sturgeon and All Fish Moon
September the Fruit Moon

October was always called the Travelling Moon as the entire tribe would relocate to the Winter Camp at Communipaw, away from the frozen river and icy shoreline.

November was the Harvest Moon,
December the Moon of Snow
January the Bitter Moon
February had the distinction of being the Moon of the Talking Trees. The ice on the trees near the river would crack loudly just before the Spring thaw in March, and the month of February was always looked forward to, and preceded the coming Spring, and greening of the entire landscape by the Great Spirit.

The Lost Lenape language also included numbers, and as on most other systems, it is based on the fingers of a human hand for counting.

N'GUTTI	ONE
NISHA	TWO
NACHA	THREE
NEWO	FOUR
PAL ENACH	FIVE
GUTTASCH	SIX
NISCHASCH	SEVEN
CHASCH	EIGHT
PESHKANK	NINE
TELLEN	TEN

ELEVEN WOULD BE TELLEN SAC N GUTTI (TEN AND ONE) TWELVE WOULD BE TELLEN SACN NISHA (TEN AND TWO) AND SO ON UP TO NOSSINACK WHICH WAS TWENTY.

This was the accomplished hand counting language of trade, and was made by holding up the fingers of both hands and touching them. Touching Leaves also explained the place names of some of the local area. Many names have become corrupted over time, but many remain as a tribute to the Lenape. Our language is peppered with Lenape words for which the early settlers were given credit, but could more accurately be described as Lenape. (Mocassins, Turkey, Squash, Pumpkin, Hawk, Skunk, Racoon, etc.)

Hackensack was called AHKINKESHAKI and meant "the place of the sharp ground." Kittatiny was called KITAHTENE and meant "big mountain". HOPOKAN, now spelled differently, was still held to be the Sacred Place of the Tobacco Pipe!

Her death, at an Oklahoma reservation in 1984 became a momentous occasion for the reunion and the renewal of custom for all of the remaining Native Americans across the nation.

She was eighty four!

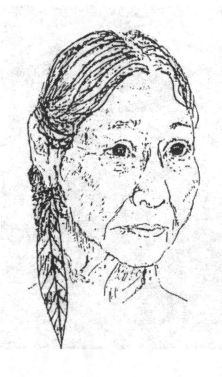

Editor's note:

Indian Mills Reservation:

The last remnant of our Hoboken Native Americans were sent, after the Treaty of Easton in 1758 to a three thousand acre reservation in Eversham County Township. The land was set aside by Governor Bernard of New Jersey, and known for a time as Indian Mills. It is now called Burlington, New Jersey.

"What is life? It is the flash of a firefly in a starry night. It is the breath of the buffalo in the wintertime. It is the small shadow that runs quickly across the grass and loses itself in the sunset."

Last words of a dying
medicine man

In this book, she lives!

M.A. O'Brien

The Indian Burial Ground

In spite of all the learned have said,
I still my old opinion keep.
The posture that we give the dead
points out the soul's eternal sleep.
Not so the ancients of these lands
the native, when from life released,
again is seated with his friends
and shares again the joyous feast.

His imaged birds and painted bowl,
and venison for journey dressed
bespeaks the nature of his soul
activity that knows no rest.
His bow for action, ready bent
and arrows with a head of stone
can only serve a life well spent
and not the old idea gone.

Thou stranger, that shall come this way
no fraud upon the dead commit
observe the swelling turf and say
they do not lie, but here they sit
Here still a lofty rock remains
on which the curious eye may trace
Now wasted, half, by wearing rains
the fancies of a ruder race.

Here still an aged elm aspires
beneath whose far projecting shade
and which the Shepherd still admires
the children of the forest played.
There oft a restless Native Queen
Pale Shebah, with her braided hair
and many a barbarous form is seen
to chide the man that lingers there.

By Midnight moons, o'er moistening dew
in habit for the chase arrayed
the hunter, still, the deer pursues
the hunter and the deer, a shade!
and long shall timorous fancy see
the painted Chief and pointed spear
and reason's self shall bow the knee
to shadows and delusions here.

Phillip Freneu

17th Century Trapper
and poet

M.A. O'Brien

Bibliography

Stevens Institute of Technology Library Special Collections Dept.

Hoboken of Yesterday George M. Moeller

The Great Explorers Samuel Elliot Morrison Oxford University Press

Narrative of the New Netherlands Jameson Reference

Jersey and It's Historic Sites 1888 Harriet Etou

Touch the Earth Hoboken Public Library

The Red Man's Continent Ellsworth Huntingdon Yale Press

Cockpit of the Revolution Basil M. Stevens personal papers

The Colony of Nova Caesaria

Hudson River Landings E.S. Winfield

The Journal of Martha Pintard Bayard Martha Bayard

Leading American Inventors Dod B. Bayard

Old Bergen by D. Van Winkle

Stevens Indicator Volume 28

The Lenape United States Department of Parks Archives

Three Hundred Years F.C. Koeler Stevens Archives

English translation of ship's logs, Shelf 43 Stevens Special Collection Department

The Palisades of the Hudson Arthur E. Mack 1844

M.A. O'Brien

The Great Explorers Oxford University Press 1888

Indian Life of Long Ago in the City of New York Bolton Press 1934

Voyages from Holland to America   David DeVries 1853
(translated from Dutch by computer)

Gleason's Pictorial   974 1886   Archive shelf Hoboken Public Library

and all of the trappers, natives and surveyors who had the temerity and the heart to record and save journals of this area.

M.A. O'Brien

About the Author

Ms. O'Brien is a researcher and collector of pioneer material of Hoboken and the surrounding area, and has penned many articles concerning the same. This is her first book.

Printed in the United States
By Bookmasters